TALES
OF
TONY
GREAT
TURTLE

TALES
OF
TONY
GREAT
TURTLE

ROGER
ROBBENNOLT

Forest of Peace
Publishing

Suppliers for the Spiritual Pilgrim

Other Books by the Author:
(available from the publisher)

Tales of Gletha, the Goatlady
Tales of Hermit Uncle John

TALES OF TONY GREAT TURTLE

copyright © 1994, by Roger L. Robbennolt

Library of Congress Cataloging-in-Publication Data

Robbennolt, Roger
    Tales of Tony Great Turtle / Roger Robbennolt.
            p. cm.
        ISBN 0-939516-27-6 (pbk.) : $9.95
        1. Indians of North America—Fiction. 2. Young men—United States—Fiction. 3. Christian Fiction, American. 4. Teton Indians—Fiction. I. Title.
    PS3568.02224T35 1994
    813'.54—dc20   94-35510
                                                                              CIP

published by
Forest of Peace Publishing, Inc.
PO Box 269
Leavenworth, KS 66048-0269 USA

printed by
Hall Directory, Inc.
Topeka, KS 66608-0348

1st printing: October 1994

cover art and illustrations by
Edward Hays

In celebration of

TONY **G**REAT **T**URTLE

who shadowed my life with storied hope

For

MADELEINE **L'**ENGLE

who unknowingly kept me writing
when despair came stalking at my door

and, as always,
for

PAT

who frees me to create
while grounding me in love

With deep appreciation to the sacred risk-takers at
Forest of Peace Publishing, particularly Fr. Ed Hays, Tom
Turkle, Tom Skorupa and Johnny Johnston—who challenge
creatively and care deeply.

CONTENTS

Come away, O human Child!
To the waters and the wild
With a faery, hand in hand,
For the world's more full of weeping
than you can understand.

The Stolen Child
—William Butler Yeats

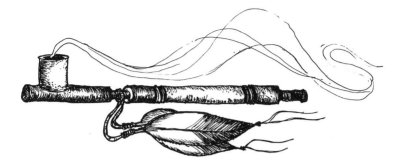

PROLOGUE

I feared the great black walnut tree, shrouded in fog or outlined against a full moon, the tips of its branches demon-dancing in a fitful wind. At times I wondered if it might be an earthly refuge for the dark star people.

Now, from the grave vantage point of a three-day blizzard-bound isolation, I watched it wavering into view through curtains of swirling snow. Its gnarled trunk seemed to writhe in the gathering dusk.

What appeared to be a large section of grey bark slid slowly into the snow. Yet when the white veil parted once more, the trunk seemed unscathed. The dark pile was slowly disappearing beneath great flakes. Folks in the neighborhood would be saying, "Mother Goose is shaking her featherbed."

It was Christmas Eve day. Bored with isolation and unamused by my Hermit Uncle John, Bible-bound in his great chair, I shrugged my way into my sheepskin coat and pulled on my high-buckle overshoes. I would bring in some fallen bark and see how well it burned in the kitchen stove as my uncle and I fried mush for supper.

I struggled to open the snow-banked door just far enough to wriggle my skinny twelve-year-old body through. I pulled the ever-present shovel out from the entryway and cleared the drift which had gathered since my last attempted exit.

I waded through the butt-deep, earth-smothering whiteness

toward the disappearing pile of bark. Suddenly, the wind quieted. Shafts of winter sunlight momentarily shattered the heavy clouds and illumined the dying day.

As I approached the tree, I noticed its trunk was still enveloped in its customary covering. The silence was marred by a groan escaping from a strange shape. It was embraced by snow and cradled in the great roots which snaked along the surface of the soil.

A roving beam of westering light paused as if to warm the shivering figure. Breath ballooned from its mouth in the frozen air. A leather hat with an eagle feather had slipped over its forehead. A leather bag was clutched by fingers clad in ragged gloves. It was Tony Great Turtle.

I knelt at his side and called his name. There was no response. I struggled shackward through the drifts calling for my Hermit Uncle John.

He appeared at the door. I shouted, "I-It's Tony. He's f-f-fallen asleep in the snow beneath the b-black walnut t-tree."

John stammered back in surprise, "G-G-Go back to him. I'll c-come to you b-b-both."

I returned and knelt by Tony. I brushed the snow off my coat and nestled his head in my lap.

My uncle's folded-in-upon-himself figure appeared at my side. He crouched in the snow, removed a horsehair glove and searched for Tony's pulse. After a moment he assured me, "His pulse is w-weak, but he's still alive. W-W-We got to g-get him inside. The temperature's d-dropping fast."

He gently lifted the limp head and shoulders. I put my arms under Tony's legs.

The light disappeared. The storm descended with renewed vigor. We slowly made our way toward the shack. The swirling snow momentarily blotted out the blaze of the kerosene lamp which John had placed in the window. It was as if night-demons were determined that the old Lakota (Sioux) holy man we carried in our arms should never find shelter.

The lamp's glow momentarily reappeared. We were indeed

off course. We moved slightly to the left and found ourselves at the entryway to the shack.

I gently lowered his feet and quickly shoveled the snow away from the drifted door. We entered and carried Tony to Uncle John's tiny bedroom.

We stretched him on the bed. I lighted the lamp on the wall. Together we removed Tony's prized black greatcoat which enveloped him to his feet. He'd told me once that it had been given to him in London by an Englishman who'd admired his riding in the Wild West Show. The label affirmed its source as a shop on Piccadilly. When he'd first showed me the address tag, I thought it said "piccalilli." It seemed strange to me that a fancy English shop would sell both elegant clothes and jars of ground cucumbers, onions, spices and vinegar which my mother put up in great quantities every summer.

Even today when I taste the pungent relish, I hear Tony's gentle laughter as he explained the difference. Echoing in the ear of my heart are the hooves of carriage horses on a London street.

We stripped off the rest of his clothes. As we wrapped him warmly in a flannel sheet, I felt like an archeologist. We'd been reading about Egypt in my seventh-grade geography class just before the blizzard stopped the school buses. Eighty-seven years had mellowed the old shaman's skin to yellow, mummy-like parchment. The scars in the soft flesh beneath his shoulder blades where the wooden Sun-Dance shards had torn him flamed in the lamplight. We stretched a crazy quilt which my ma had sewn for Uncle John over Tony's frail form. I reached into his leather medicine bag and removed the sacred deerskin. I knew he would want it to cover the altar of his dying body.

He still shivered uncontrollably. I shrugged out of my sheepskin coat and laid it gently over the old man. He quieted.

I knelt at his bedside and held him in my arms. His breath rattled ominously in his chest. Uncle John murmured as he left the room, "He needs a m-mustard plaster."

After a few minutes John returned bearing a piece of flannel smeared with a mustard-laced paste which was the local universal remedy for sickness in the chest. We lifted the covers and spread the pungent wrapping on the emaciated figure. I remembered words from the Bible about spices for embalming.

John left me for a moment. Returning with the stool he used to step up and light the high wall lamps, he stretched to turn down the wick of the bedroom light. The room dimmed to a faint yellow glow. Stepping down, he commented softly, "If you're going to be there for awhile, you'd b-b-best sit on this. You'll be more c-comfortable."

As I murmured my thanks for the gift of the stool, my Hermit Uncle John said, "I'll sleep the night in my reading chair. I think maybe you and Tony could use some time together. In the normal c-c-course of things him and me'll probably be in the same place sooner than we know."

He smiled for a moment and then continued, "I've always h-hoped when I get to where I'm g-g-going after the g-gift of death comes, I'll b-be able to talk to special folk without st-st-stammering."

He slipped from the room.

Sitting down, I opened my heavy wool plaid shirt and the top buttons of my long winter underwear. I laid the old man's icy cheek on the warm flesh of my bare chest.

Suddenly, Tony struggled upright. He choked out, "I see them coming down the hill: Longhair and the bluecoats. They're heading for the village, loading rifles as they ride."

A long wail broke from his lips as he sank back on the pillow.

Through the next five hours I alternated between my memories of moments when he had saved me from the dark star people and his hallucinatory images from the depths of his soul which always began with a chant growing out of other chants:

O Cody!
Longhair Bill Cody!
How many times must you kill my people?
How many times must you kill my heart?

BREATHING IN THE STARS

I hated milking cows. The task was always related to darkness. I would struggle by lantern light into the predawn world with my silent father. In fair weather the morning star would mock me, poised as it seemed to be on the beak of the rooster-shaped weather vane atop the barn roof.

Sometimes Dad would leave me by myself to strip dry the teats of the reluctant beasts while he fed the rest of the livestock. When the weather was freezing, I'd blow on my hands before stroking the cows' udders. Cold fingers would assure a swift kick which would knock over the bucket, spilling the hard-won milk. Often the raging hoof would connect with the milker's leg as one sat crouched on a three-legged stool. A painful cloven bruise would remind me for days of my raging father's attendant comment: "Stupid, careless kid!"

My daddy was sick in his mind—which is just about the worst place a person can have a sickness. There were those moments when he was loving and playful and caring. He would have unlimited energy. If a neighbor needed help, my father would be the first person on the scene. Everybody in the vicinity of Pheasant Valley loved Frank Robbennolt.

At times, however, without warning, he'd spiral down into what my mother always called his "darkness." This would only happen when he was home.

On the way down, his anger flamed out. He'd use anything

within reach as an instrument of abuse against my mother and me: his fists, a horsewhip, a pitchfork. The horrific strength that accompanied his illness would occasionally drive him to tear a thick limb from a tree and beat me to the ground with it. Exhausted, he would sink soundlessly into an old oak rocking chair in the living room and creak out the duration of his depression. If anyone would come to the isolated farmstead, we'd secret Dad in the back bedroom or guide him quickly to an outbuilding hidden in the thick grove of elm trees behind the house. My ma wanted to avoid the shame of having other folks know that we had somebody "sick in the head" as part of our family. Three or four times a day she'd remind me that I was "never to tell anybody."

My father's constant companion during these episodes was our black-and-white mongrel dog, Skippy. He'd curl up at Dad's feet and wait for him to rise, walk to the barnyard and throw a corncob or a stick for him to chase.

All of a sudden, Dad would rise from the chair and be filled with that unnatural energy which would drive him ultimately back into depression.

At those times Mother would escape the terror by going off for extended periods to "help out" folks with sickness in the family or a new-birthed baby.

I would retreat to those beautiful outcast people who were derided by the rest of the world but who held me and kept healing available to me. There was Gletha, the goatlady, when I was a small boy in northern Minnesota. Now there was my Hermit Uncle John and his mysterious frequent visitor, the old Lakota shaman, Tony Great Turtle.

I loved my daddy in his all-too-rare moments of tenderness. Then, with absolutely no warning, he would brutalize the affection out of me, leaving within me a roiling pool of hate.

The results of my daddy's darknesses had blighted my soul for nine years. My parents had taken me out of an orphanage when I was just over three years old. That first night in the unfamiliar house with those two strange people, he had slapped me to the floor because I'd touched the battery-operated radio. He feared I might turn it on accidentally and run the batteries down so he couldn't listen to "The Lone Ranger" and "The Six Fat Dutchmen Polka Band" which he always said gave him "a lot of comfort."

I kept wishing John and Tony and Gletha could hold Dad and sing out songs of healing. He consistently rejected them as crazy people who were trying to steal his son away from him.

That was my worst agony: the fierce conflict between love and detestation on the battlefield of my heart. Tony and Gletha and John tried to keep me on a path toward compassion, forgiveness and, yes, even toward love. I guess the fact that I can write these stories means they were partially successful.

My daddy had strong feelings about every aspect of my behavior. One of his mandates was spelled out with particular force: "Boy, you are not to waste yer time playin'. There ain't no time in this damn life to play if we're ever goin' to make it without starvin'. It's bad enough havin' yer ma sittin' on her butt crocheting them stupid antimacassars when she oughta' be makin' quilts to keep us warm when the snow flies. There's always plenty of work to be done. Jist don't let me catch you readin', neither. That's the same thing as playin'."

I was scrupulously careful never to play or read when there was a chance he might be around. However, after surveying the landscape within the barn, I occasionally played a game while milking.

My partner in the crime of joy was a three-legged black cat. Her birth defect never fazed her. Being fascinated by mythology I'd named her "Medusa of the Mice." She was the best mouser on the farm. Any unfortunate grey rodent would first be hypnotized by her scary, steady stare and then attacked with such fury that she seemed to have twenty paws instead of only three. She gave lie to any sense that disability spelled dysfunction.

She would line up her mangled trophies on the back step of the house so that we would have to admire her skills. There was much "good kittying" and ear scratching as reward.

If my father was not present at milking time, Medusa would crouch about four feet from my stool. I would aim the cow's teat at the cat's mouth and strip an expert stream across the intervening distance.

Sometimes I'd miss on purpose. Medusa's night-toned fur would become beclouded with white. She'd slink off to a corner to lick herself clean. Then she'd return for more of the game.

One late afternoon, I thought I'd checked to make sure that Dad had not returned from town. I failed to hear his car. Just as I was letting fly a stream of rich milk toward Medusa's waiting mouth, his clenched fist struck my cheek with incredible force, knocking me facedown into the urine and manure-filled gutter behind the cow. Stars exploded behind my eyes as I slipped into momentary unconsciousness.

When I came to, I saw a gigantic shadow projected on the barn wall by a beam of sunlight breaking through a grimy window. I watched in fascination as the shadow s-l-o-w-ly bent down and picked up an inert body by the straps of its bib overalls. Holding the limp figure like a great rag doll, the shadow spoke: "I think you must be deaf, boy. Here we are on the way to the poorhouse, and you waste precious milk and cream on that damned cat. How many times have I told you not to play?"

The shadow's voice got louder. The world came into sharper focus. I realized that it was me that was being dangled from the clenched fist of my angry father. His voice dropped to a whisper: "I guess I'm gonna' hafta' do something else to teach you not to play."

He set me on my feet. I wobbled as he shoved me toward the empty horse stall next to the milking alley. Picking up my three-legged stool, he followed me. I thought maybe he was going to make me sit on the stool. Then he'd nail the door shut and just leave me there until I'd "learned a lesson about never playing."

Instead he placed the stool carefully against the far side of the stall. He looked up at two empty pegs extending from the barn wall. They normally held horse collars. He shifted the stool slightly to the right so that it was precisely between the pegs.

He turned to me and softly spoke his most dreaded words: "Strip, kid."

I shucked out of my overalls and stood shivering before him in the intense heat of a barn in late July. He looked me up and down. A strange little smile played at the corners of his mouth. I thought he was laughing at the mask of manure stains on my face. He muttered softly, "Yuh jist wait a year or two. I'll really teach yuh somethin' that'll keep yuh in yer place."

Raising his voice, he commanded, "Step up on that there stool with yer back to the wall."

I obeyed.

He reached to a hook on the far side of the stall and removed a shining coil of new hemp rope. Tying a slip-knot in one end, he stepped over to me. He grabbed my left hand and thrust it through the loop. He yanked the now-looped rope tightly around my wrist. I winced. It felt like a hundred tiny needles thrusting into the soft flesh.

He threw the free end of the rope over the pegs above my head. He jerked on it. My arm felt as if it were being torn from its socket.

He quickly lifted my free arm and wrapped the dangling rope around the wrist. He shoved his knee against the barn wall between my bare legs. Levering his foot on the stool, he sharply lifted me while tightening the rope. Pain exploded in my groin.

Removing his knee, he dropped me down. Muscles tore in my shoulders. The soles of my feet barely grazed the uneven surface of the worn stool. He bent down and moved it forward just beyond the reach of my searching toes.

He stepped back and looked at me appraisingly like a landscape painter evaluating his art. He grinned approvingly at the picture of his manure-stained, naked son dangling from horse collar pegs on the stall wall.

I stammered out, "D-D-D-Daddy, don't l-leave me here. It hurts s-s-so bad. I p-promise. I'll n-never, n-n-never p-play again."

He replied slowly, softly, "Yuh just hang there quiet-like, boy, and think about that promise."

Leaving the stall, he slammed the gate. Sound exploded through the barn like a rifle shot. Pigeons fled from high rafters and escaped through a hail-shattered window high in the hayloft.

Silence settled, broken only by occasional mooing from unmilked cows whose distended udders made them uncomfortable.

I looked up. In the last shaft of late-afternoon sunlight illumining the wall above my head I was terror-stricken to see a great black spider stalking my left hand. My fingers halted their futile efforts to escape the binding rope.

The creature crawled slowly into the palm of my hand. I thought it might inject me with venom as I'd seen its cousins do to flies caught in their webs. At least I'd be out of my misery. I momentarily envisioned my inert body as a banquet site for a million tiny spiders.

With great precision the spider began spinning a web in and out through my fingers. Its legs brushing my flesh felt like fine sand in a dust storm.

Sweat cascaded down my body. Tiny rivulets of blood oozed from my tortured wrists. The longer I hung there, the harder it became to breathe.

A picture flashed across my mind. When eight-year-old Manfred Tollerson was gored to death by the Pillitzer's prize bull, everybody went to Manny's funeral. It was held at the Roman Catholic Church of St. Ignatius the Lesser in Pheasant Valley. My mom almost broke my ribs with her elbow when I got to sneezing as the incense was lighted.

The service was real long. Father MacCarrity was as old as Adam—at least that was the general opinion among the young of the town. He'd stride down the street, his black robes bellowing in the wind around his large-framed body, well over six feet tall, his long white beard flowing to one side, his enormous mustache mountaining above a mouth from which came the voice of doom. Whenever he encountered kids under fifteen, he'd step in front of them, pinion their attention with his soul-boring grey eyes and thunder out the same question in his basso profundo voice, "Have you been good today? God will love you if you have."

He never waited for an answer. As he swept on down the street distant children would magically evaporate in order to avoid the sacred confrontation.

As the service lengthened toward late afternoon, I decided to focus on pictures in the stained-glass windows. There was one of Jesus hanging on the cross in just about the same position I was in now. I was surprised that Dad had not chopped off a length of rope and put it around my head. The needled hemp would have made a fine crown of thorns.

Somebody'd at least had the decency to put a cloth around Jesus' middle so he could die modestly. If anyone had happened into the stall, I'd have had no way of covering "my shame" as my daddy always called my genitals.

There was another stained-glass picture of our Lord being put in a cave behind a big rock and a picture of him heading upward on a cloud. I had no idea where he was going. I guessed it was probably to heaven.

As I hung gasping on the wall, I wished God would send a cloud to take me away. I remembered the priest proclaiming that Manny would one day rise as a spiritual body with no sign of the bull's horn tearing his flesh. How I wished I had that kind of body right now. I couldn't bear the pain of the one I had much longer.

My theological reverie was shattered by loud, persistent meowing. I looked down at the stool. Medusa of the Mice was looking up at me, demanding that I come down and finish both the milking and her dinner. She couldn't seem to understand my helplessness.

In the distance I heard a low rumble of thunder. One of those sudden late-afternoon storms was rolling across the plains of southern Minnesota.

The squall quickly drew near. The torrent of rain mixed with hail pounded on the barn roof. Through the high window I could see lightning tearing the sky. It reflected off the wall above my head.

There'd been lightning around the cross in the stained-glass window. Maybe God *was* sending a storm cloud to carry me beyond my sick daddy's brutality.

A horrendous crash of thunder tore the world. I writhed in fear. Medusa panicked. She leaped from the stool. The force of her three departing paws slid it slightly toward me and knocked it in such a way that it leaned precariously against the wall.

I touched it gently with my toes. Could I get the proper leverage to slide the rope from the pegs? One misstep and I would die on the barn wall with no real assurance of divine cave or cloud.

I put a bit more pressure on my toes and raised myself slightly. I flicked the rope off the collar pegs. At the same moment the stool slipped. I crumpled to the straw-littered floor. I did not have within me breath enough to sob.

The fury of the storm abated, leaving only a gentle patter of rain. The stall grew lighter. I felt something rough moving across my left cheek. Turning my head slightly, I saw that it was the black cat ministering to my needs with her tongue.

I struggled dizzily to a sitting position. I removed the rope from my clotted left wrist. I discovered that in the process of my fall the spider had been crushed in my hand. I freed my other wrist.

I staggered to my feet, picking up my overalls as I rose. Keeping a hand on the wall for balance, I stumbled out of the barn. The cold rain revived me. I let it wash the urine, manure, dust and blood from my tortured body. I held out my overalls so that they might be cleansed as well.

As the water cascaded over me, anger rose within. I wanted in the worst way to kill my daddy. But years of being assured that I could never do anything right forbade my attempt for now.

I pulled on my soaking overalls. I headed over the fields toward my Uncle John's protective shack in the woods on the shore of Lake Sumach, a Lakota holy lake.

The old hermit was my father's brother. He would be there to hug me. He always was. He knew the meaning of terrible interior pain. His closest friends had died at his side in the mud and blood and bullets of the Great War in France. The terror of that time haunted his tongue so that he stammered just like me. He was driven to live by himself—except for a pet skunk named Pity Me, a little dog, Tiny, and a shelf full of the best books in the world in matching red leather bindings.

The rain stopped. The sunset sky blazed with reds and golds. The first stars appeared.

I ran along the wooded path in the gathering dusk. The rain-weighted leaves caressed my face. Arriving at the cabin, I called out for John. There was no response. At evening time he usually visited his "spirit friends" on Shaman's Point. Perhaps I would find him there.

I walked to the rear of the cabin which nestled against a great granite outcropping. I followed a narrow path to the top. As I climbed, anger again overcame me and I sobbed.

Stepping up onto the rock's extended flat top, I realized I was not alone. The song of the twilight breeze was joined by another whose high-pitched harmonics blended perfectly with the wind's soft wail and the mourning doves' calls from the meadow. I recognized that second melody. Through my tears I saw a familiar figure silhouetted against the blood-red sunset sky. An eagle feather rose above the curved brim of a worn leather hat. The ancient body was clothed in familiar faded denim. It was Tony Great Turtle.

Beneath each arm Tony carried a skull. I was not surprised. My Uncle John lived near a site where the Lakota had placed their dead on great platforms. After being exposed to the healing elements, they were placed in the earth. As John expanded his garden, he often dug up bones.

Tony Great Turtle would instruct us to bring the bones to the tip of Shaman's Point and leave them for three days in the sun and the rain and the moon and the stars. Then we were to place them once again in the earth within the sheltering roots of the great black walnut tree.

He now laid the skulls gently on the soft moss which grew on the edge of the rock, nourished by moist breezes from the lake.

Looming before Tony on the opposite high-banked shore of the narrow cove was the Baptist Church of Peter-the-Rock. Its slender steeple was topped by a huge, out-of-proportion, ungainly iron cross which looked as if it might keel over at any moment, carrying the church into the waiting waters below.

He lit a fire in a small pit which had been chiseled out of the rock ages before. I was a little surprised that he used an ordinary match to light it. The mysterious red fire at the tip of Shaman's Point seemed often to flare on its own, keeping the surrounding neighborhood in a state of astonished awe.

Tony tenderly lifted the skulls while crooning an ancient lullaby-like dirge. Smoke caressed them. His song wavered in the wind. It died out for a moment, then rose again to join the twilight lilt of meadowlarks.

From my vantage point it looked as if the skulls rested on the arms of the distant cross. For a moment I saw the One who had hung there reach out his arms. He embraced at once the old Lakota shaman, my Hermit Uncle John, my beaten mother and my fear. I wondered if I would ever come to see him embrace my mind-sick daddy.

Then I remembered my crucifixion on the barn wall. My anger burned brighter inside me than the red fire on the rock tip. I fled down the narrow path. I didn't want to see anybody or be touched by anybody. I was overcome with a desire to destroy as I had been destroyed.

I hid in the hazelnut bushes where the path left the rock. I waited a long time. Finally the old man chanted his way by without acknowledging my presence.

At odds with my anger, I climbed back up the path. Each step accented the rage roiling within me. I tore leaves from offending bushes that had the audacity to brush my face.

As I stepped out onto the rock, a flock of ravens arcing high in the sky were silhouetted against the dying light. They settled into the black walnut tree below with uncharacteristic silence. I was observed by a hundred intense eyes.

A sliver of moon squinted at me from just over the eastern horizon. There seemed to be fewer stars than usual. Perhaps they'd dimmed themselves in the face of my anger.

I stepped past the still-glowing embers of the red fire which illumined the intense whiteness of the skulls nestled in the moss at rock tip.

I lifted the objects of death together. I examined them with clinical detachment. A clean hole front and back through the skull on my left suggested a bullet's passage. The forehead of its companion was battered in. Had the two been brothers in battle and met their deaths in differing ways?

Whatever they had done in life they were absolutely worthless now, just like me. My daddy was right. I was no good. I might as well be dead like the remains in my trembling hands.

Then I felt an aliveness about me. Were the "spirit friends" of Tony Great Turtle and Hermit Uncle John hovering around me with an intensity I could sense in the marrow of my living bones? Perhaps the spirits of the men whose life-cases were now at my mercy were asking for gentleness from me to balance the violence which had originally snuffed them out.

The slivered moon rose behind the cross on Peter-the-Rock, faintly silhouetting it. In my whirling mind the One from the stained-glass window was mounted there. He seemed to have forgotten his own agony and was straining toward me as if to embrace me.

With that vision the pain and the anger from my afternoon ordeal rose with an unbearable sharpness. My shoulders flamed. My wrists itched. They were bleeding again. I lifted my left hand so that I might rub them together. I was stopped by blood dripping on white bone, sharpened in red firelight.

I stepped to the very tip of Shaman's Point. My bare toes extended beyond the rough granite into empty air. I raised my tortured arms. The pain from the horse stall burned redder than the nearby fire.

Swimming through my tears, the bullet-riddled skull in my left hand assumed the features of my adoptive daddy. The skull in my right was fleshed out with the unknown face of the man who had made the terrible mistake of fathering me in the first place.

With all my remaining strength I flung the skulls downward. A moment later I heard them explode on the jagged rocks of the lakeshore.

Torn by sobs, I looked toward the cross. Was the figure really weeping? Was its body bowed out toward me? If I leaped from the rock tip, would He somehow catch me in his arms and carry me away from all my pain—or would I explode on the rocks below? Either alternative seemed better than where I found myself at this moment.

I crouched, prepared to spring from the rock. I was stopped by a sound. The incredible music of soft running water washed over me. The cool green of meadow streams and the murmur of a river beneath winter ice touched the heat of my anger. Woven into the sound was a song I had heard many times:

Tunkashila, hoye wayinkte.
Namahon yelo
Maka sitomniyan
Hoye wayinkte.
Mitakuye obwaniktelo.
Epelo.

Grandfather, a voice I will send,
Hear me!
All over the universe
A voice I am sending.
With my relatives I shall live.
I am saying this.

Tony had followed me up the rock, removed his rainstick from his medicine bag and was angling it gently back and forth. The sacred beads and pebbles and seeds flowed around the cactus needles which had been driven into the slender two-foot piece of desert vegetation.

I collapsed backward on the rock, exhausted by my anger and drained of all will to live or die. My body clothed in still-damp overalls was torn by fierce shivers so severe that my head bumped out of control against the rock.

The old man, still singing, knelt beside me. He opened his medicine bag and removed his sacred deerskin. He covered me with a gentleness I'd observed in a neighbor man blanketing his newborn daughter. Tony put the soft bag under my head.

Reaching beneath the deerskin, he unbuckled my overalls and gently massaged the abused muscles in my shoulders. His song changed. Over and over again he chanted in English:

Father, Great Spirit,
Behold this boy!
Your ways
Shall he see!

As he sang the red fire flared warmly, its heat calming my shivering body.

He removed an abalone shell from his medicine bag along with a twist of sweet grass and a pouch of sage gathered in the sacred manner. He placed a pinch of the herbs in the shell, picked up a small dry stick which he lighted from the red fire and ignited the contents of the shell. Intoning a Lakota chant, he fanned the smudge with the eagle feather from his hat. He offered the shell to the west, the north, the east, the south, Mother Earth and Grandfather Sky. Then he crossed my battered body with the healing incense.

I looked up at the night sky. The stars were now shining with a peculiar brightness. The Big Dipper hung directly overhead. My eyes were drawn up the pattern of the heavenly ladle till I found the North Star. I could not pull my gaze from its gleam.

After a long time, Tony paused in his massaging of my shoulders. His song faded to a whisper, to be replaced by the rustle of the rainstick.

He spoke softly. "The night-stars reveal the darkness deep

down within you. Your daddy keeps pouring more and more in and you keep hugging it to you and hating yourself and the whole world in the process. Boy, I think you need to be in touch with the stars."

I responded hesitantly, "I think maybe I need a star inside me."

His low chuckle joined the laughter of the water sound in the stick. "You've got one there. *Wakan Tanka*, the Great Spirit, created light within every creature before he slipped it into the world. You've just got to find yours again."

"How do I do that?"

"All you have to do is breathe in the stars."

That idea was so scary that for a moment I stopped breathing altogether.

Tony continued, "Focus your eyes on the heavens' brightest star. Take a long, slow, deep breath through your nostrils. As you breathe in, let the voice of your heart sing:

Starlight
Return within me.

"When you slowly release your breath through your mouth, let the voice in your heart sing:

Darkness
Flee to the west.

Tony timed my breathing to the rainstick's rhythm. I slowly inhaled, inviting in the light. As my breath flowed out I begged the darkness to depart.

As I lay suspended in space on Shaman's Point, staring at the night sky, thousands of stars seemed to flow to the Dipper's ladle and pour from there on the stream of sound into the depths of my soul. There was more and more room for them as the darkness fled.

I slept.

I awakened to the first faint sunrays in the east driving the morning star from the sky. Before she disappeared, I automatically "breathed her in" with the heart song. As I exhaled, I sensed the darkness rushing to join the night as it disappeared westward.

I was aware of Tony stretched out at my side under the edge of the deerskin, one arm over me protectively, his head nestled by mine on the medicine bag.

The incense of frying bacon rose up to the holy place from the cabin of my Hermit Uncle John. I rolled carefully out from under the sacred skin and rose stiffly from the rock. As I rose, my unbuckled overalls slipped to my ankles. I stood for a long moment reveling in the light within and without.

I stared at the steeple of Peter-the-Rock. The figure from last night's vision seemed to be fading with the rising of morning. Was He smiling?

Tony stirred. I pulled up my overalls and buckled them. He smiled at me. I gave the old man a hand up. I knelt down and packed rainstick and deerskin in the medicine bag.

We walked silently downward. Tiny, John's black-and-white fox terrier, skittered up the path and leaped into my arms. She licked the salty tearstains from my cheeks.

As we stepped into the cabin, my Hermit Uncle John was putting the finishing touches on a breakfast feast. A shaft of morning light illumined the table. The egg yolks in the center of the circle of crisp bacon returned the sunlight's rays.

Not a word was spoken. We fell immediately into comfortable communion.

Tony and I stepped to the sink. He filled the wash pan with warm water from the reservoir on the end of the cast-iron cookstove. I was admiring the beautiful brown of the thick slices of the world's best homemade bread toasting on the stove lids.

My reverie was broken by Tony firmly applying to my face a rough washcloth fragrant with the mint of homemade soap. He commented, "I just thought I'd hit a few spots Tiny missed."

The three of us sat down at the table. Without a word we joined hands. Tony intoned some words which emerged into English:

A dawn appears: Behold it!
Light
Dance within us.

Having gorged myself on my uncle's largess, I slipped away from the table. Pity Me, Uncle John's pet skunk, emerged from my uncle's bedroom where she always slept in the pillowed place of honor. Later, I would take her out and romp for a bit in the morning sun. I felt an overwhelming need to play.

I paused in the main room of the shack. The walls were covered with my Uncle John's handiwork: shields woven from straw, reeds and cattails. Intricate designs made from hundreds of arrowheads were attached to them. The largest image was the pictograph outline of a thunderbird. It seemed to be staring directly at me. I couldn't pull myself away from its gaze. As I stood there I was overwhelmed by a sense that I had one last ritual task to perform.

I paused in the entryway and picked up a beautifully woven basket which John used to gather tomatoes, walnuts and gooseberries. It too was resplendent with a thunderbird woven in dark fibers on its side.

I walked down to the lakeshore. I circled toward the jagged rocks beneath Shaman's Point. A granite upheaval blocked my passage. I would have to wade out into the lake to reach my destination.

I couldn't swim. I was afraid of deep water. My daddy had tossed me from his wooden fishing boat a couple of times, expecting that I would automatically keep myself afloat. I floundered to the point of drowning until he, in great disgust, retrieved me.

I slipped out of my overalls, clutched the basket tightly and stepped into the holy lake. Fed by countless springs, its waters were always chilly.

I waded slowly, exploring the underwater terrain with my bare toes. Just before reaching my destination, I stepped into a hole and plunged to my armpits. I gasped and fought my way to level sand.

Just ahead I could see the shattered bits of bone glowing in the early morning sunlight. I tenderly picked up each piece and placed it in the basket. I sensed singing in the air around me. Were the Lakota "friends" gathering in a ritual of forgiveness for my act of anger? I searched long and carefully, picking up every fragment I could find. I waded back through the lake to the shore. I paused for a moment to let the warm sun and lake breeze dry me. I donned my overalls and, picking up a shovel from the shed, headed to the great black walnut tree.

The flock of ravens alighted above me. They were strangely silent. I dug a deep pit between the exposed roots.

I stepped to the nearby garden and stripped some wide leaves from a cornstalk. I lined the grave with them.

As I reached into the basket for the first bone shard, a high-pitched dirge sang out. I turned. Tony Great Turtle was standing near me, sounding his eaglebone whistle.

Bit by bit I emptied the basket. When I completed my task, I gently sifted dirt over the white bones. Having filled the hole, I rose stiffly to my feet. With a raucous song of celebration the ravens exploded from the tree.

Pity Me appeared and rubbed against my bare feet. I picked her up, snuggled her for a moment and headed to the barn for a game of hide-and-seek. Finally, I was free to play.

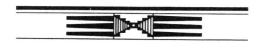

INTERLUDE 1

The old man in my aching arms stirred. The wind mourning in the branches of the black walnut tree brought me back to the holy night. I shifted my position slightly. A sound arose, a high-pitched dirge echoing through his nostrils up and down the scale. His feet moved beneath the deerskin as if he were ghosting through a gentle dance.

His lips shaped sounds: Lakota phrases rhythmically trickled out. English words began to fleck the stream of sound. I put my ear close to his lips. Phrases repeated over and over shaped themselves into a consistent chant:

O Cody!
Longhair Bill Cody!
How many times must you kill my people?
How many times must you kill my heart?

Snow lay heavy in the valley late in the Moon of the Popping Trees (December)...each evening sleep came to the song of a stream singing beneath the ice.

On this wakan night my mother prayed for birth through pangs of pain...neighboring women walked through scarlet light toward the sounds of her moans...my ten-year-old feet fled fast from the teepee.

In the last rays of the westering sun I followed the stream toward a beaver dam...water roar at dam site drowned the sound of their coming...the long line of bluecoats casting shadows on snow...the white soldiers holding rifles at ready...Hetchetu welo! (It is so!)

At their head was a man whose hair flowed long in the light wind as he rode a fine cream-colored stallion...curled in the bushes beneath my buffalo skin, I knew the great horse who looked to my hiding place but made not a sound...I'd loved him at last summer's Sun Dance...he had belonged to

Chief Tall Bull of the Cheyenne...I could not take my eyes off the great beast and its rider...I wished to be like them...horse and rider together. *Hetchetu welo!*

One day, riding by, Tall Bull swept me up with him...as men often did...to encourage small boys in their dreams of the hunt...we rode to the edge of a vision mesa...the great horse quivered on the sacred ground...Tall Bull spoke quietly..."*Wakan Tanka* revealed your sacred name to me...*Wakan Tanka* has holy work for you." *Hetchetu welo!*

I was frightened...holding me for a moment, looking deep in my eyes...wonder words flowed: "The Great Turtle...Spirit of birth and long life...swims in your soul's center."

We rode back to the dance lodge like the roar of the north wind...he lowered me to the ground, saying, "Earth Mother, receive your sacred son"...I did not understand him...I watched him ride off...he was soon to be slaughtered at Summit Springs. *Hetchetu welo!*

Soldiers paused at the stream...removed mallets from saddlebags, breaking the ice so that they and their horses could drink...they were talking loudly...my Mandan mother, who had lived with a white family, taught me the language of the whites, the *wasichu*—"the takers of the fat"...the longhaired one assured them they were quite near the village of the wagon train killers...I wished to cry out that our people were peaceful...they had destroyed no one. *Hetchetu welo!*

I slipped like a weasel through the dense bushes and ran toward the village...our teepee was first on the stream edge...my father stood silent, face toward the heavens, awaiting the birth of his child...I whispered my message...a quiet warning breathed through the camp.

My father was assured by women in the tepee that birth was some time away...he knew of a hillside cave where bear cubs were born...he wrapped my serene mother in a buffalo robe...followed by one woman we moved quickly to safety...from the cave's mouth we looked down on the village shining in moonlight, quiet in starlight.

Gun barrels flashed as warriors circled...then to our terror we saw horseless soldiers creeping through forests high on the hillsides surrounding the village...two bluecoated *wasichus* knelt in the snow just below us...one of them mourned, "It's a hell of a way to spend Christmas Eve."

A single shot shattered the crisp winter air...all the soldiers fired together...screams from my people answered the hail of bullets...warriors, surprised, could sight no targets...a tepee flamed up...in its light our chief lifted the white flag of truce.

Warily, soldiers closed in on the village, firing shots in spite of the flag while shadowed figures fell to the ground.

Hoofs sounded on the frozen earth as soldiers brought horses...at the forefront rode Cody...Longhair Bill Cody... sweeping into the camp like a grand kingly conqueror...his subjects stared at him silently...stared at him hatefully...a wild weeping rising for the twenty-one killed: men, women and children. *Hetchetu welo!*

Behind us another cry cut through the air masked from the soldiers by the crying of women...my father disappeared through the low cave entrance...I crept quickly after.

In the dance of a small fire's flames I saw my crouching mother, a babe at her breast: my infant brother...my father's shadow leaped large on the wall, a hovering figure offering protection...the attending woman breathed pleas to the Great Spirit.

I slipped outside...the evening star hung low...its rays reaching toward the cave mouth....Cody moved to the shadows at the edge of the village...he was watching the star...Soldiers were clustering my people together...laggards encouraged by blows from rifle butts.

Longhair rode royally stage center...knew our language in word and in sign...his voice cut through the cold air..."We march tomorrow...no more will you need to steal and burn...you will live out your days cared for on reservations by the Great Father in Washington"...the words meant death: death to our wandering, death to our ways...the weeping rose louder. *Hetchetu welo!*

O Cody!
Longhair Bill Cody!
Generations have passed
And I must forgive you.

The English phrases became interwoven with Lakota until he sang a song to release his soul. In the midst of the melody, the old man fell asleep once more in my arms.

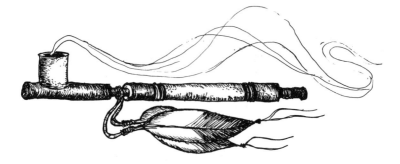

LIFE JOURNEY, DEATH JOURNEY, LIFE JOURNEY

He sat in the great oak rocking chair. I stared at him illumined by the first rays of dawn. My daddy had been sitting there for two days, except for those times when he rose from his chair to follow the worn path to the two-seater nestled in the lilac bushes. In late spring the heavy odor from the lush blossoms masked the stench rising from the rank shack.

He had been sitting in the chair so long that the wounds on my mother's arm where he had jabbed her with a pitchfork had already begun to scab over. When Margita Williams asked her about the bandage, she responded quickly, "Them wasps built a great nest in the haymow. I was throwin' down some feed for the stock, and three of 'em dive-bombed me on my left arm right together-like. I just bound some blue mud onto the stings 'til they heal."

I noticed that she did not look Margita in the eyes as she spoke. When you have to lie in the name of love—or for any other reason—you keep your dignity by looking away.

This whole cycle of violence and silence had been my fault— as usual. It had started at milking time Tuesday last. A lot of my memories, good and bad, seem to be born in a barn.

I really disliked milking Old Dora. This gigantic Holstein cow was Dad's prize milker. She was also an evil-tempered, dangerous bovine blindsider. You never knew when she was going to munch hay placidly while you cautiously stripped the rich liquid from her teats or when, out of the blue, she would fire off a swift kick, knocking the pail into the gutter or splitting the skin on the milker's leg.

I was afraid of Old Dora and she knew it. Sometimes my daddy would put a hobble around her rear legs to protect me. More often than not he would grumble, "She looks pretty calm tonight. I'm not going to use the hobble. If you did yer job right, I'd *never* need to."

As I warily moved toward the end of my task I heard my mother enter the barn. One of the hens was trying to nest in the horse stall. Each evening Mom would gather the deposited egg.

Just as I rose from my three-legged milk stool, Old Dora released a tremendous kick. She missed my leg but connected with the brimming bucket. It upended. Before the milk was completely absorbed into the layer of crushed straw on the stall floor, a cadre of cats appeared as if from nowhere and licked up what they could.

My daddy was forking hay into the manger. He heard the dull clang of hoof on metal. He rushed into the milking alley. Angry disbelief spread over his face. He shouted, "You careless bastard! You've done it again. Yer stupid clumsiness has cost me a bucket of the richest milk in Sunrise Township. What do I have to do to get you to remember to be careful around Old Dora?"

He was standing in front of me, his face in mine. As he shouted, he waved the pitchfork menacingly.

Mom rushed in, demanding, "Frank, leave the boy alone. Ain't nobody can control that crazy beast."

Dad retorted, "Mary, you keep your distance. This damned kid is nearly old enough to be a man. I wonder when he's going to start acting like one."

She kept coming toward him as if to pull him from me. He jabbed the pitchfork toward her to frighten her away. He misjudged his distance. Three tines struck her arm. She screamed and backed away. Blood spurted from the wounds. She fled sobbing from the barn.

With no sign of concern for her, he returned his attention to me. "Look me in the eye, boy."

I dragged my gaze from my bare feet to his angry steel-grey eyes. He continued, "I keep thinkin' I'll find some way to jog your memory about doin' important things right. Maybe if you feel a little pain every step you take you'll remember caution."

Without taking his eyes off mine, he lifted his heavy steel-toed boot and crashed it down on the bare instep of my left foot. Pain shot through my entire body. I swallowed my scream but could not hold back the tears which broke my focus on my father's eyes.

He turned slowly away. His shoulders slumped forward as he leaned the hayfork against the wall and stepped out into the gathering dusk. I knew that darkness was gathering inside him as well.

I looked down at my throbbing foot. It had begun to swell. I watched in fascination as the tattoo-like tread of my father's boot ingrained in my flesh slowly expanded. I half dragged and half hopped to the pump in the farmyard. I managed to flow enough water across my burning foot to quiet the fever.

Mother stepped out of the house, saw me and scurried across the sparse grass. Tears riveted the summer dust on her cheeks. She said, "He's creaking away in his rocking chair. Did he hurt you bad?"

I replied, "N-No worse than usual. He just d-d-did in my foot for awhile, but I'll b-be okay. Y-Y-You're the one he really hurt. Shouldn't you be got to the doctor s-s-some way?"

"No, I just wrapped it good. I keep my lockjaw shot up. You jist never know what he'll do next."

Now, two days later, as I stared at my slumped daddy, the dawn light deepened to a brilliant red. His balding head appeared bloodied. My eye strayed to the poker standing by the wood-burning heater, cold in the warmth of June. For a moment the vision of his skull bashed in by one swift blow from my strengthening arm gave me a sense of belated justice for his brutality. I wondered, if I killed him would somebody dig up his body fifty years from now and think he'd been attacked by a savage wielding a tomahawk?

Mom bustled in with some ice wrapped in a washcloth. She leaned his head back against the chair. As she put the cold compress on his forehead, she informed me, "Sometimes this helps bring him out of one of these terrible fits and silences."

I was nauseated by her caring. I said abruptly, "I've g-got to get out of here. I think I'll head for L-L-Lake Sumach."

She responded quickly, "Well, don't you catch no fish. We got more'n we need already."

"Maybe I'll j-just go and sit qu-quietly on the shore."

She retorted, "Well, just don't ever let yer daddy catch you doin' nothin'. He'll have your hide for sure."

I limped out into the penetrating light of the early June morning. The pain in my foot reminded me of my general worthlessness—at least in the eyes of my father. Then I saw it—Venus, the morning star, fighting its losing battle with the rising sun. I quickly breathed in its light before it disappeared into the encroaching day. For a moment I felt at one with the rising sun and the winging meadowlarks. I realized that when stars disappear, their transforming warmth need not be lost.

I crossed the fields and bits of forestland that stood between our house and Lake Sumach, the holy lake. Silhouetted against the sky I saw Mark Mannfield plowing his early corn. As I crossed the end of his acreage, I noticed that the new plants appeared in disciplined rows like snippets of green velvet. I paused for a moment to touch one of the unfolding leaves. Years ago Gletha, the goatlady, had stroked my finger across the surface of a moccasin flower, reminding me that it felt like a baby's cheek. The young corn carried the same kind of hope.

I laughed to myself as Mark moved exactly across the face of the rising sun. Just before school let out for the summer, Betty Markey brought a shadow puppet to our class. Her brother had sent it to her from Sumatra where he was fighting in the Great War.

Our sixth-grade teacher, Miss Collinger, had rigged a light and a sheet. She mounted the puppet on a stick, and we watched its shadow dance. That's exactly what Mark looked like.

Mark was always nice to me. A half-dozen years older than I, he'd dropped out of high school when his dad fell into a threshing machine and was killed. He decided to run the farm and try to take care of his mom and two younger sisters. Sometimes I'd stop by and help him with haying or digging potatoes. I wished I was his real brother. He'd put an arm around my shoulder and tell me I was a fine worker. For a little while his voice would drown out my dad's shouting which ceaselessly echoed inside me.

Sometimes he would appear at my side as I fished in Lake Sumach. He would often have his throw line coiled in his hand. If I was there, he always knew I'd have more than enough angleworms for bait buried beneath moist soil in my Campbell soup can. If I was nearing the end of my supply, he'd disappear for a few minutes. He'd go to a pile of manure, carefully lift a layer of the decaying bounty and quickly gather fat cream-and-brown grub worms.

I turned my eyes away when he baited his hook. You could hear a tiny staccato explosion as the barbs penetrated the grub. The chubby sunfish and crappies seemed to swarm to this deceptive feast. Sometimes if my luck was extra good, which it was most of the time, I would give him my surplus catch since he had a lot more mouths to feed than I did.

If the day was particularly warm, he would slip out of his clothes. Standing for a moment on the edge of the rock, unashamed of his body, he would let the healing breeze from the holy lake caress him. Then he would knife cleanly into the water, scarcely disturbing it. He knew every rock and drop-off in the entire lake. I would watch his astounding grace as he somersaulted again and again just below the surface, holding his breath for incredible lengths of time.

One day I didn't know he was anywhere around. All of a sudden my fishing bobber plummeted out of sight. I felt a great pull. I was using a throw line and could hardly bring it in. A few feet from the shore the surface was shattered by a rising head of tightly curled brown hair with a bobber in its mouth. It was Mark.

He often tried to coax me into the lake. He promised he would teach me to swim. I was terribly afraid of the water because of my dad's forcing me into it. Mark would put an arm around my shoulders and assure me that someday I would lose my fear. I hoped I could tear my attention away from it long enough to lose it.

As I now crossed the fields, Mark spotted me and waved. His hand danced like a great black moth on the orange face of the rising sun. I waved back and continued my slow, painful journey.

I entered the lakeside woods. Tiny usually dashed out to greet me. There was a thick silence hanging over the heavy stand of trees. I shouted, "Uncle J-John, are you around somewhere?" There was no answer.

I decided he was probably driving his cows to the far pasture. I walked on down toward the lakeshore and stepped out onto the great flat rock from which the Lakota had launched their fishing canoes. I loved to sit right on the edge and dangle my feet. I was eager to do that this glorious morning. Maybe my foot would be healed in the mysterious waters.

The moon, just setting, appeared to be playing hide-and-seek with the rising sun. I lost myself in the dance of light as an erratic breeze ruffled the surface of the water. Dragonflies swooped. They appeared to be riding on beams of light rather than air currents.

My reverie was broken by the sound of whistling in the distance. There was no mistaking the raw energy of the tune. Its source was Ben Bittergraven.

Ben was two years older than I and a head taller. He was the village braggart. According to him, he could run faster, throw a ball harder and beat up more of his fellows than any other boy in the environs of Pheasant Valley. He kept his face and feelings masked by a frozen expression that was half sneer, half grin.

One day he bet Bartie McCale a quarter that his "manhood" was bigger than Bartie's. Ben turned to me: "You can come with us out to the woods and be the judge, Rog."

Since I was never a part of the gang, I was surprised and pleased to be invited to do anything—even when I wasn't quite sure what it was.

I followed them into a little glen thickly screened by hazelnut bushes. They stood facing each other about six feet apart. I stood uncertainly near them. Ben said to me, "Okay, Rog, give us a slow count of three."

I gave them a slow count of three. Together they dropped their pants and undershorts. What sprang up from Ben's groin was truly amazing. Bartie's penis seemed to shrink practically out of sight from sheer embarrassment.

He quickly pulled up his pants, reached into his pocket and wordlessly handed Ben a quarter. Then he fled red-faced through the forest.

Ben stood gloating in the woodland shadows, every inch a conqueror. He proclaimed, "Now you know what a real man looks like, at least where it counts most."

I mumbled, "S-S-See y-you l-l-later" and quickly followed Bartie before I was invited to participate in the competition.

Ben's taunting laughter followed. He shouted, "You two will never be men!" I cringed as I ran. I'd heard the same words over and over again from my father.

Now, on this bright June morning when everything seemed brilliantly alive, Ben broke through the bushes and strutted out onto the launching rock. He greeted me with, "Hey, Rog! Whatcha' doin'?"

I blurted out, "I was j-j-j-just sittin' here w-w-watchin' the sun on the w-water."

Ben looked at me in amazement: "You mean you weren't doin' nothin' ceptin' that?"

"N-n-n-no."

"Well I'll be—I don't think I've ever seen nobody doin' nothin'. Rog, you're kinda' strange. But you know, you ain't all bad. You weren't afraid to come to the woods to judge Bartie's and my little competition the other day. Too bad there was no contest."

The lakeshore rang with his raucous laughter.

I'd pulled my damaged foot out of the water and drew my knees up to my chest trying to make myself as small as possible. I never knew what his noticing me might lead to.

Ben stretched out catlike on the rock in front of me. He stared at my swollen instep. He reached out his right index finger and traced the print of my father's boot. I felt as if my skin was being caressed by goosedown.

He whispered, "What happened to your foot? Yuh look like yuh bin run over by a tractor!"

I countered quickly, "Oh, n-nothin' much. I just sprained it a little."

"That's some 'little sprain.' Did yuh get that the same way yuh got the black eye two weeks ago...the same way yuh got the big bruise on your arm a month ago?"

Without thinking I shot back, "How d-d-did you know about that b-bruise? I always wear long sleeves when I-I-I got one."

Ben's face softened. His deep-set brown eyes searched me as if he were a doe concerned for her fawn. He responded, "I was behind yuh in line at the boys' room sink. Yuh'd just come from art. Yer hands were covered with red and blue chalk. I wondered if you'd gotten any on the paper at all. Yuh rolled up yer sleeves to wash. I saw a red and blue welt down yer arm. At first I thought it was a smear of chalk dust. Then I looked closer. Chalk marks don't fester."

I was overcome with the enormity of what I'd said and done. Ever since my parents had adopted me when I was three, my mother told me over and over again, "Don't you tell nobody that yer daddy's sick in his mind and hurts us. It's shameful if you got somebody sick in their mind—at least that's what all the neighbors'd think.

"If he was thought to be real bad they'd carry him away to the crazy house in Wilmar and dump him in the loony bin."

The first time she said it a picture framed itself in my mind. My daddy and a whole lot of other folk were in a padded room. Moonlight flooding through a barred window eerily striped them. They were talking together in those mysterious voices which the loons used on northern Minnesota lakes while Gletha was teaching me to hear God's voice in them. I wondered in passing if Dad wouldn't be happier in such a room.

Now I'd opened our family's secret to the whole world. Ben would blab about it to everybody as he bulldozed his way through the world.

He was staring at me strangely. For an instant I felt as if I were drowning in his gaze. Then he offered me a strange invitation, his voice breaking as he spoke: "You want to see something, Rog?"

In the stark intimacy of the moment I was afraid he was going to leap up and drop his pants again and expect me to do the same. Instead, he simply lifted his chin. The sun rays intensified the contrast of the white flesh beneath his chin and the bronze of his face.

At a point just below his Adam's apple there was a deep bruise. Four lesser bruises girdled his neck on either side.

I stammered out, "Wh-what h-h-happened, B-Ben?"

"Last night I was sittin' in the living room playin' a game of Old Hogan's Goat with my three younger sisters. Ma was turning a collar on a shirt so the wear wouldn't show so bad. Dad came in raging drunk. The girls and I started to leave. He told us to stay where we were. He grabbed Ma. She tried to pull away from him. He slapped her hard and told her never to try to get away from him again. The girls were sobbing. He told them to shut up—that he was going to show us the only thing a woman was good for. He started to undo his pants with one hand while holding her by a wad of her dress with the other.

"I jumped and grabbed him by the hair, trying to pull him away. He swung around and clutched me by the throat hoping to strangle me. He was too drunk to do much damage. I managed to swing on him and connect a solid left to his cheekbone. He dropped like a ton o' bricks.

"The girls were cheering and clapping and whirling around the room like water bugs in a stock tank. I herded them to bed.

"When I came back, Ma'd blowed out the kerosene lamp. Headlights from a passing car swept through the window. I saw her crouched on the floor with his head in her lap. I could see she was rockin' him. I heard her singin' to him somethin' about, 'Momma's gonna' buy you a diamond ring.' I slipped out the back door, vomited and just run and run and run, nowhere in particular."

Tears were streaming down Ben's face. I moved closer to where he was still stretched on the rock. I pulled his head into my lap. I didn't know the song about momma and the diamond ring, but I would have sung it to him if I did. He shifted his position slightly. Unthinkingly he rested his wrist across my battered instep. Sharp pain flowed up my leg. I didn't move.

He asked quietly, "So what's wrong with your dad. He doesn't drink, does he? I never see him around the Dew Drop Inn."

The dam in my soul was broken. Words flowed as quickly as my stammer would allow. For a few moments on the launching rock we shared that which was more deeply private than mere contests involving body parts.

I questioned Ben: "Wh-What are you g-g-going to do about y-your hurtful dad?"

Ben shook his head sharply like a spaniel emerging from the water. He was emerging from an unexpectedly healing country of the spirit he had never explored before. He couldn't stand it.

He pulled himself brusquely away and stood up. He had withdrawn behind his usual mask: half smile, half sneer.

He exploded, "Boy, I don't know what got over us, sharing all those secrets like a coupla' stupid girls and hangin' on to each other right out in public. Geez, we sorta' got all emotional there for a minute. I guess I'd better get at what I came here to do. Uh, by the way, don't worry about me tellin' nobody about this. It'd be just too embarrasin'."

A door in my heart slammed shut. I asked, "Wh-wh-what was you gonna' do?"

The old braggadocio returned. He rose grandly from the rock and announced, "Today is going to be a red-letter day for me. I've taught myself how to shoot a gun, drive a tractor and wrestle. I got up before the sun this morning and cleaned the chicken coop and spread the manure on the garden. I decided that now I'm going to relax in this here water and teach myself how to swim."

I replied quickly, "B-B-Ben, you're crazy. There's deep holes all over this l-lake. I d-don't know h-h-how to sw-sw-swim. At l-l-least, don't go in until there's s-somebody around to p-pull you out if you get into any t-t-trouble."

Ben's great laugh circled the shore once more as he quickly slipped out of his clothes and folded them in a pile on the launching site. He paused for a moment, looking over the cove to the Baptist Church of Peter-the-Rock. He made no overt attempts to show me again what a real man looked like. He said with a mocking air, "Helen Jepson, the old lady evangelist, is in town with her tent meeting. As I ran by last night, she was shouting something about Jesus bearin' you up in the waters of life. I guess I don't have nothin' to worry about. Old Jesus will just carry me around the waters of the lake."

He jumped off the end of the rock. Half floating, half dog-paddling, he thrashed his way noisily toward the flattop ridge of granite that rose out of the water marking for everyone who knew the lake the beginning of its deepest point.

Ben climbed on the ridge and shouted back to me, "Well, I've made it this far, so I must know about all there is about swimmin'. I shall now instruct myself in diving."

He went headfirst into the water. He splashed wildly for a moment. Then I could no longer see him. The top of his head rose momentarily like a distorted fishing bobber. Then it disappeared once again beneath the surface.

The realization struck me that Ben was in desperate trouble. As usual, I was absolutely useless. I had to go for help. If Uncle

John were home, he might take his rickety old boat out to help Ben. It was too heavy for me to handle alone. I shouted for my uncle. There was no answer.

I knew what I had to do. I had to run for Mark as fast as I could. He was the best swimmer in the township. My pace was slowed by my clumsy injured foot.

I arrived at the field where he was cultivating corn. Thankfully, he was at my end. He was taken aback by my shouting onslaught. I was almost too winded to make clear what had happened. He finally comprehended, handed me the reins of his horses and told me to tie them to an oak tree by the gate in the woven wire fence.

Mark took off running. I admired his graceful passage. I tied up the horses securely and ran as best as I could back to the lake. When I arrived, there was a second pile of clothes on the launching rock.

Mark was knifing through the water at great speed. Arriving at the ridge where I had last seen Ben, he stood up briefly, scanned the water carefully, and dove far out from the rock.

He reappeared, caught great breaths and disappeared again beneath the water. It was on his fourth reappearance that he was pulling Ben behind him. Even from a distance there seemed to be no movement from the young would-be swimmer.

Mark pulled him up on the distant rock and stretched him out on his back. I saw him kneel over Ben, doing everything he could to make him breathe again. I looked up to the tip of Shaman's Point towering over them. If some of the "spirit friends" from the Point could be alerted, perhaps they could assist in bringing breath to Ben.

After a long time I saw Mark slump. He remained motionless. He slipped from the rock and rolled Ben's body into the water after him. He towed the burden behind him like a funeral barge. There was no doubt in my mind that Ben was dead.

When Mark swam up to the launching rock, he rested his arm on the edge, put his exhausted head down and sobbed. I didn't know quite what to do. Mark finally climbed out and together we eased Ben's body up onto the rock. We stretched him on his back. It was then that I saw the great gash in his forehead. Mark said he had not dived far enough out from the granite outcropping to avoid its shallow extensions beneath the surface. The necklace of bruises seemed to glow on his pale, waterlogged flesh with a kind of life of its own.

My legs would no longer hold me up. I sank to the rock and buried my face in Ben's dark hair and cried out my anger, my grief and my disappointment in myself. Dad was right. I was no damned good. If I hadn't been afraid of the water and had learned to swim, if I could have run faster on my injured foot, this would not have happened to Ben.

It didn't seem quite right somehow to leave Ben lying naked on the rock while we went to call Undertaker Turlow. We struggled him into his shirt. Mark lifted him at the waist so I could slip on his shorts and his pants. I observed that in death his "manhood" was no longer dominant.

Ben's funeral was held the following Tuesday in the Baptist Church of Peter-the-Rock. Ma stayed home with Dad who was still in his darkness. Both my Hermit Uncle John and Mark accompanied me to the service. We passed by the open plain pine box laden with lilacs. Undertaker Turlow had done a fine job concealing the wound in the forehead through the art of makeup. He'd made no attempt to hide the glowing neck bruises.

Ben's father, Trap, had been too drunk to shave. He stood, scraggly bearded and smelling of booze, staring into the coffin. He kept shaking his head as if trying to figure out just who was lying there. Ben's mother remained semi-conscious in the family pew. His sisters wept in the arms of neighbor women.

Ben's dad sat down next to his wife for a few moments. Then, just before Pastor Phil mounted the pulpit, Trap Bittergraven stumbled forward to the pauper's box which held his son's remains. From my seat in the second row, I saw Trap lift his shaking hands and with infinite tenderness place the tips of his fingers in proper order on the bruises. His body was torn by sobs. He bent over and kissed his son on the forehead. When he lifted his head, a jagged gash of flesh-colored makeup distorted his mouth. He turned and staggered down the center aisle and out the church door. It was later reported that he headed straight for the Dew Drop Inn.

Mattie Conners, proprietress of Conner's Corner Bar and Grill, sang "Rock of Ages" in her quavering high soprano. She was always half a beat behind her accompanist. Since Ben had been killed by hitting his head on a rock, I questioned the appropriateness of the selection.

From the vantage point of my pew, I could see through the window a triangle formed by Shaman's Point, the launching rock and what would come to be known in the neighborhood as Death Rock. I wondered if Ben's spirit would join the "friends" around the Point and somehow find release from the terror in which he had lived.

Pastor Phil stepped to the pulpit and read some words from the Bible:

> Who shall separate us from the love of Christ? Shall tribulation, or distress, or persecution, or famine, or nakedness, or peril, or sword? As it is written, for thy sake we are killed all the day long; we are accounted as sheep for the slaughter. Nay, in all these things we are more than conquerors through him that loved us. For I am persuaded that neither death, nor life, nor angels, nor principalities, nor powers, nor things present, nor things to come, nor height, nor depth, nor any other creature, shall be able to separate us from the love of God which is in Christ Jesus our Lord.

He flipped the pages of the Bible and continued reading:

> Let not your heart be troubled: Ye believe in God, believe also in me. In my Father's house are many mansions: if it were not so, I would have told you. I go to prepare a place for you. And if I go and prepare a place for you, I will come again, and receive you unto myself; that where I am, there ye may be also. And whither I go ye know, and the way ye know.

I sat puzzled. I liked the bit about nothing separating me from the love of God. I did think whoever wrote down the words of Jesus about mansions and such must have missed some of it. I had no idea at the moment where Jesus was going, or where I was going, or Ben was going, or anybody else was going. I was sitting here looking at a boy in a crude box. I needed to be shown a little more clearly where hope really lived.

Pastor Phil assured the packed church that Ben would be raised a spiritual body and be held in the everlasting arms of God. I wished we could have had one more time of sharing our private griefs and holding one another in a healing way.

Both Mark and Uncle John had their arms around me. I didn't really understand about the everlasting arms of God. Being embraced by the two people I was closest to was the next best thing. I wondered if maybe it was the same thing.

I managed to hold back my sobs. Mark broke down as we processed past Ben for the final viewing. I knew that he too carried a sense of failure inside himself. I squeezed his hand real hard. Uncle John guided us out the back door of the church.

When Ben's coffin had been put in the ground of Pheasant Valley Cemetery, I had my Hermit Uncle John take me home with him. I told him I didn't want to talk about anything to anybody. He respected my silence.

It was nearly sundown when I sat on the launching rock, letting my tears flow as they would. The emotion I felt most keenly was an overwhelming loneliness. Ben and I had come together for one wonderful trusting moment. Now that was impossible to discover again.

From the depths of my despair, I heard a sound behind me. At first I thought it was only the wind rustling the leaves of lakeside willows. For a moment it sounded like a great flock of birds in flight. Then the tones of flowing water entered the counterpoint of sounds.

I turned quickly. He was standing in the shadows. In his hand Tony Great Turtle was tilting his rainstick slowly back and forth. The cactus branch with its spines driven in and filled with sacred beads, pebbles and seeds sang a soothing song of moving water and earthgrown sounds.

He walked toward me, the eagle feather in his leather hat outlined against the setting sun. He sat down wordlessly beside me, continuing to let the rainstick's lyric voice sing alone.

Finally he said, "John tells me that you have encountered sorrow. Tell me about it."

Words came tumbling out. The rainstick had for the moment erased my stammer. I explained how the whole incident was really my fault, how if I had learned to swim I might have saved Ben, if I hadn't done something dumb and made my daddy hurt my foot I could have run faster, and how maybe by sharing my troubles with Ben he had been so weighed down that he couldn't have swum if he'd known how.

My daddy had taught me well. My paean of self-laceration reached new heights. Suddenly, in the roughest voice I'd ever heard him use, Tony shouted at me, "STOP! That's enough of your nonsense. How many times have you been assured that you are a beautiful person in the eyes of *Wakan Tanka*, the Creator Spirit. The world may tell you that you're worthless. It is not the fault of your father or anyone else if you believe the lies you are told.

"I am sad. I have enveloped you in sacred smoke and taught you to breathe in the stars. And yet such a one as you believes the lies of the troubled world. I *am* saddened."

A night chill was settling in. Tony removed his deerskin from the medicine bag and draped it around us. After a time of silence he said, "If the death of Ben troubles you so deeply, I think we should head up to the tip of Shaman's Point."

Tony handed me the rainstick. I shifted it gently. The sound of falling rain and running water was answered by raincrows in the meadow. I felt at one with myself and the golden sunset world surrounding us.

We climbed the narrow path. The glory of the evening burst upon us. The red fire was already glowing in the ancient pit. I didn't even ask Tony if he'd been here earlier.

We folded the deerskin and sat down on it. He said, "Tell me everything you know about Ben and about Ben's death. Tell it to me without any mention of your supposed responsibility or your supposed worthlessness. It would be good for you to do a complete soul cleansing."

I paused for a long moment. Then I ventured a problem with my soul cleansing: "I promised Ben I'd never betray the secret of his pain. I'll feel real guilty if I tell you. The last thing in the world I need is to feel guilty about anything else."

A quiet smile played on Tony's lips. "You are telling it only to me in this most holy place after his death. You need not feel guilt."

I poured out every detail to Tony. To my surprise he chuckled when I told him about the "contest" in the woods, and he muttered something about boys at play. I told him about our pact never to share a word about the pain we lived with. I wept as I shared my real grief: how I'd just discovered a friend who might keep promises and he was snatched away from me.

Tony corrected me: "He was not snatched away from you. He made foolish decisions which caused his journey to turn a corner before it needed to. Boy, I think you know very little about death."

I responded quickly, "All I know is that it's real scary and I don't want to meet up with it right now."

Tony chuckled again and said, "That proves that someone has given you a lot of misinformation about death. My great-grandmother who trained me to be a shaman—to be deeply in touch with all that is spirit in all—told me this about death—and I am convinced it's true. She said that life and death are part of a single journey. They are one and the same. When what we know as death happens, only the scenery changes."

I sat mesmerized by his voice and the gold-dappled heavens and the rainstick which he reclaimed and began to make sing to accompany his words.

He repeated, "Always remember and say over and over to yourself, 'Life and death are part of a common journey. Only the scenery changes.'"

I wondered what kind of scenery Ben was looking at right now. Tony had an answer for that as well: "We don't worry about others' scenery. They have created the patterns for it in their lives in this world. But *Wakan Tanka* assures us that we can *really* live in the world when we round the sacred corner. Patterns will no longer destroy."

I wasn't sure what it all meant, steeped as I was in the imagery of heaven and hell. But I felt a calm returning to my spirit.

Tony looked at me with a twinkle in his eye. He said, "I will teach you a song to help you remember that you never need be afraid of death."

I brightened. He was always teaching me exotic Lakota chants. He then would tell me what they meant in English. At first I wanted him to teach them to me only in English. He assured me that their power would be lost if sung first in a language other than their native tongue.

I settled down against Tony, ready for the long, arduous process of absorbing a new chant. He began to hum a variety of wordless melodies. Finally, one emerged which I thought I recognized but was unclear in the midst of the syncopations and mood changes in Tony's music. Suddenly, he began to sing in English—to the tune of "Happy Birthday"—these simple words:

> *Happy journey to you,*
> *Happy journey to you,*
> *Happy journey, dear Ben,*
> *Happy journey to you.*

We sang it again and again until my heart echoed it without my lips. Tony reminded me one last time, "Whenever you remember a person who has gone on that journey called death, sing the song over and over. When anyone is sad, give them this melody. Grief has difficulty overcoming a heart which sings."

Tony started into the little chant once again. It seemed louder this time. Our good "friends" on Shaman's Point had joined the chorus.

INTERLUDE 2

Tony's body was torn by an involuntary spasm. I tried to hold him more closely. He jerked himself awake.

He turned and looked at me in the dim glow of the lamp. He said weakly, "I'd like a bit of water for my lips."

I removed my arms carefully and rose stiffly from the little stool. As I stepped into the kitchen, I saw that my Hermit Uncle John was sleeping in his great chair, *The Complete Works of William Shakespeare* open in his lap.

I took down my special glass from the kitchen cupboard. It was bright blue with the milk–white image of the child actress Shirley Temple emblazoned on its side. I lighted the dipper from the water bucket which I'd pumped full mid-afternoon and filled my glass for Tony.

As I entered the room, his eyes were open. He was staring at the light from the kerosene lamp. I put an arm around his shoulders and lifted his head. I moistened his lips. I tried to get him to take a full drink.

He refused with the words, "I don't want to do anything to hold off the visit from my new guide, Death."

He paused, becoming silent for a moment, and then added to his first request: "Leave the water in the glass. Tomorrow, after I have completed my soul's journey, pour the water on Mother Earth as a 'thanks gift' from me in return for her reaching out in my last hour and giving of her bounty to soothe my lips."

I sat down by him, promising to make his special gift. I laid my head on his pillow, my cheek next to his. I sensed his body temperature was dropping. I dozed.

I was awakened by his singing. The chant alternated between Lakota and English:

Grandfather, behold me!
Grandfather, behold me!
I have given you the offering of my life,
That my people may live!
Grandfather, behold me!
Grandfather, behold me!
I who represent all the people,
I journey toward you,
That we may live.

He was quiet for a moment. Then a jumbled narrative broke from his lips:

O Cody!
Longhair Bill Cody!
How many times must you kill my people?
How many times must you kill my heart?

The blizzard broke on the holy day...all were forced to march through the blinding snow...my family returned to our tepee in the very early morning...starvation would have followed if we dwelt in the secret cave...Cody's great stallion nickered in the background...I knew he remembered my sacred ride on his back...if only we could have ridden off the mesa and into the arms of the Grandfather. Hetchetu Welo!

Our two horses bore my mother, sheltering my infant brother, and my frail great-grandmother whose eyes burned with hatred for the man on the cream-colored stallion...I led one and my father the other.

The forced march to the reservation moved through the blizzard...the weakest left to be covered by the snow's gentle blanket.

My great-grandmother called to me while we paused to rest the bluecoat's horses...I helped her to the ground and held her as she whispered: "Our life way is cast out by Longhair and the bluecoats and the guns...know this, my little shaman...wakan cannot be destroyed from the skies and from the hills and from all living things...the rocks beneath our feet are wakan...the bluecoats bear their wakan if they are ever quiet enough to sense it...no, wakan cannot be destroyed...it can only be ig-

nored." *Hetchetu welo!*

"*If you keep in touch with* **Wakan Tanka** *and touch the earth and all living things with that* wakan *born within you, you will plant the seeds of hope that may one day even root within the* wasichus.

"*In its rising and its setting the sun will ever show you the presence of the holy...you must raise your head...if they forbid you to lift your voice in ancient song, your heart can sing...sing without ceasing:*

> O You, Power there where the sun goes down:
> You are a relative,
> O You, Power, where the Giant lives:
> You are a relative.
> O You, where the sun comes from:
> You are a relative.
> O You, Power, there where we always face:
> You are a relative.
> Heaven: You are a relative!
> The Earth is our relative."

Her voice fell...she whispered:

> To Her I go now with a smile on my face,
> To Her I go now with a smile on my face,
> To Her I go now with a smile...

Her whisper went silent with a long sigh of air...the tiny woman fell limp in my arms...Bill Cody passed on his great stallion...pausing, he called out, "Need some help with her, boy?"...I dropped with her snowward, covering her with my body...I stared up at him, refusing any words...he shook his head sadly...rode on down the line of marchers.

My father knelt beside me...took snow in his hands, held it toward the north chanting:

> In this Moon of Popping Trees
> You, Thunderbird, gift us
> With snow to nourish growing things.
> Now Thunderbird,
> Enfold the spirit of your holy woman
> With your wings.

He sprinkled snow upon her face...we left her in the Spirit's care...I mounted on her horse...felt the Great Turtle's presence in me. Hetchetu welo!
We rejoined the weary plodders...moving toward our bodies' degradation and our souls' imprisonment.

O Cody!
Longhair Bill Cody!
Generations have passed
And I must forgive you.

Tony was racked by a fit of coughing. I stroked his throat. He rested while my memory wandered into story, evoked by his mention of Great Turtle.

THE TURTLE

I wasn't sure I wanted to dabble around in people's blood. But that seemed to be what we were headed to do in my Hermit Uncle John's ancient truck. I was uncomfortably sandwiched between him and Tony Great Turtle as we jounced along rutted back country roads.

We had gotten up in the middle of the night because Tony said we had to be where we had to be before sunrise. An incredibly bright star led us westward. In order to keep awake I hummed under my breath "We Three Kings of Orient Are." We were on our way to encounter mystery. I knew I was in the company of two wise men. I thought it was entirely possible that one of the original magi was a confused kid in training.

A sliver of moon followed us. Uncle John drove slowly and carefully to avoid the skunks and raccoons who made the gravel ribbon their playground. Jackrabbits occasionally danced a wild ballet in the headlights.

Tony sat hunched in his corner, eyes closed, chanting in his native tongue. He would open his eyes at odd moments to give Uncle John directions. We were not driving the straightest of routes. Tony said he was following the path to the most sacred place taken by him and his great-grandmother when he was a child a few years younger than I was now. I asked him once how he knew his way in the dark. I assured him that if I'd known we were going to be wandering around the countryside in the dead of night I would have "borrowed" my daddy's compass which he took with him into the woods when he went hunting deer. Tony said he was being guided by a spirit compass inside. I let that comment pass without further questions.

We were headed for a city called Pipestone. I'd heard of it all of my life. I knew it was a lot bigger than Pheasant Valley. When local farmers couldn't get what they needed in nearby towns, they'd drive "all the way to Pipestone" to purchase a part for a tractor or threshing machine. This was always said in a tone of voice that made it sound like they had gone to the edge of the world. As we continued our odyssey in the dark, I thought that was exactly what we were approaching.

This journey had begun on Shaman's Point the previous afternoon. Life had been going surprisingly well for me. Dad had not slipped into a darkness for six weeks or more. There were moments when he whistled or laughed. I thought we might even get to the point where he would tell me that I had done something real good.

Dad was headed into town. I asked him if he would drop me off at the end of the long driveway that led from the county road way back in to my Hermit Uncle John's. He looked at me strangely—he could never bring himself to speak a civil word to his emotionally war-battered brother. He assented, however, even saying I could spend the night if I wanted to.

I walked down the long lane. Sunlight danced on the distant waves of Lake Sumach. I paused at my uncle's shack. His pet skunk, Pity Me, was asleep on the front step. I looked through the window. John was nowhere to be seen.

The day was bright and beautiful. I was feeling like the day. I headed up the narrow path to Shaman's Point. I saw two men sitting silently on a long bench-like outcropping of granite just back from the tip of the Point: my uncle's hunched form and a figure topped by a leather hat with an eagle feather.

Unaccustomed silence on my part seemed in order. I slipped onto the bench by the side of Tony Great Turtle. Neither of the old men acknowledged my presence. I nonetheless felt totally accepted: at one with them and the mysterious invisible "friends" with whom they seemed to be communing.

I don't know how long we sat there. We were beyond time. The early afternoon sun seemed to stop in its journey. We focused our attention on the dancing light and the song of the soft wind counterpointed by the occasional voices of ravens or robins or red-winged blackbirds.

I slowly became aware that Tony had laid a large, calloused hand on mine. I looked at him. He was smiling down on me.

He broke the silence with an affirmation: "I sense rare joy inside you. Your daddy has found peace for the moment. You are feeling that Rog is good. Perhaps you should tell yourself that."

I tried to answer him. The words wouldn't come.

He mused, "To speak well of yourself is a foreign language. Try on these simple words: 'I am good.' See how they feel."

I painfully stammered out, "I-I-I-I am g-g-g-g-"

I couldn't get the word out. A cacophony of voices screamed inside me: my father's assurances that I was "no damned good," teachers reprimanding me for coloring outside the lines, playground denizens teasing me about my buck teeth and my stammer.

My Hermit Uncle John reached behind Tony and put his hand on my shoulder. I tried it again. The word "good" floated out without a trace of a stammer. The sound stifled the interior voices. I felt I had become as transparent as the "friends" who inhabited the great rock. I was floating free over the holy lake.

Tony squeezed my hand and chuckled: "I think you have just taken the first step on your vision quest."

"My what?" I asked without a trace of a stammer.

"Your vision quest—your journey toward discovering who you really are."

I thought I knew who I was, but I decided this was not the moment to pursue it. Tony descended back into himself. Talk and time were suspended once more.

I was jolted back to the present when he lifted his hand from mine, bent over and opened his medicine bag which rested on the rock at his feet. I knew some of its contents: a sacred deerskin, an eaglebone whistle, a rainstick, an abalone shell, sage gathered in the sacred manner and a twist of sweet grass.

He knelt on the rock, spread out the deerskin and began to chant. He slowly removed a small object wrapped in red cloth bound with buffalo sinew. He gently placed it on the sacred skin. Removing the abalone shell, he opened his pouch of sage and sweet grass, mixing a bit in the shell. Taking a match from his pocket, he lit the dry leaves. Then he detached the eagle feather from his hat and fanned the shell until the richly scented smoke rose up. As he always did, he lifted the shell to the west, the north, the east and the south. He elevated it to *Wakan Tanka*, the Great Spirit over all. He touched it to Mother Earth who embraces our every step.

He crossed himself with the smoke. From long experience, Uncle John and I knew that we were about to share a particularly holy moment. It would not be right to have unclean persons present. We knelt on either side of him. He crossed each of us with the earth-scented incense.

He lifted the tiny packet off the deerskin and slowly unwrapped it. He held the small object in the palm of his hand. Taking the eagle feather, he fanned the burning herbs into a rich smudge. He passed his hand through the incense and offered the object to the pattern of holy places.

Then he lowered his hand so that Uncle John and I, properly cleansed, could view this most sacred of objects. It was a small worn turtle that had been carved from some kind of dark stone. I was amazed that Tony had performed all this religious rigmarole over a mere turtle. Mud turtles and snapping turtles were forever impaling themselves on my hooks, particularly when I fished nearby Massacre Slough. I looked at the little beast and then at Tony with wrinkle-nosed disdain. He penetrated my immature response with a glance that went straight to my heart.

I covered my discomfiture with a question: "Does the little turtle have something to do with your name?"

"It has more to do with my life lived between earth and

sky, with a center to my wandering, with the spirit who connects me to all spirits."

I was dumbfounded. How could an ugly little object in the palm of his hand mean all that kind of stuff? Then I noticed, looming over his left shoulder, the cross on the steeple of the Baptist Church of Peter-the-Rock just over the cove. It occurred to me that an ugly hurtful thing *could* stand for a whole bunch of good things.

Tony drew my eyes back to his. He continued, "My great-grandmother slipped this little turtle into my parents' tepee the night they came together. The Lakota understand that when the turtle's sacred image is present at the coming together of a man and a woman, a son will be born. Nine months later I came into the world.

"On the day of my birth, the old woman took back the ancient turtle."

I interrupted, too quickly as usual, "How did you ever get it back?"

Tony didn't answer. He began a quiet chant, rose to his feet and stepped to the very edge of the Point. His movement was so graceful and his song so haunting that I half expected him to float out over the water.

He elevated his hand toward the westering sun. His song intensified. Three white gulls in flight, seemingly mesmerized by the melody, settled on the distant cross. He turned slowly to his awed human audience.

Out of the Lakota rhythms and phrases emerged his story shaped in English: "My great-grandmother healed at this sacred site. She traveled back and forth to the Dakotas, but this was the place of her long ago people. Fields and forests, lakes and rivers and holy places sustained her tribe before they were driven west by the whites, the *wasichus*.

"She could not forget her ancestors buried here and her present scattered family who would return to this lakeshore to live and to die. Her spirit was alive in her people who fought the final battle for their sacred sustaining lands here on this lake and around Turtle Pond which the *wasichus* renamed Massacre Slough.

"She brought me here when I was twelve. I was to be 'Carrier of the Story'—the story that would allow our people to remain in touch with *Wakan Tanka* no matter what happened.

"She had trained me in many sacred ways of the four-legged world and the plant world and the two-legged world. She sent me here to Shaman's Point alone one dark November after blessing me with shell and pipe. I was to remain alone until I received a message from the spirit world assuring me of who I was meant to be.

"As I left her in the woods where John's cabin now stands, I saw her place an abalone shell in a forked branch which she planted in the middle of the path to the top of the rock. It was a sign that no one should disturb me.

"I remained in prayer for seven days of sunlight and sleet and early snow. I left my body standing naked except for a buffalo-hide robe and a sacred deerskin. My spirit quested among the very stars. There were dark star people who tested me. They attacked me with whips and knives made from comets' tails and broke me apart with destroying lies about who I was and who I might be. They twisted me in terrible torment until I feared I must return before I knew my name. I cannot tell you everything that happened.

"I felt lost among the star clusters. When I was about to give in to despair, it appeared: a great turtle who took me on its back. The dark star people stared in wonder as I passed through them. The longer I rode the holy plodder, the taller I became. Finally I twisted beams of light from the full moon into a great spear and flung it into the midst of my enemies. They burst into flame. The Great Spirit, pleased with my bravery, made me a promise: the charred bodies of my enemies would drop through the heavens eternally. Even now in the night sky you can trace an occasional flaming fall of a dark star person.

"At dawn on a brilliant November morning the great turtle swam down the beams of the morning star and left me here.

Then he dove into the waters of the holy lake. Great waves rushed back and forth as he frolicked. I watched as the great turtle rose up and rode back to heaven on the path of the setting moon reflected in the water.

"I lay exhausted on the rock in a deep sleep. I awakened to the smell of sweet grass and sage. Great grandmother was passing the smoke across my weakened body. She knelt beside me, saying, 'I dreamed of you night after night while you quested. And this is what I dreamed.' She repeated all that had happened to me in the heavens.

"At last she said, 'I gift you with your birth turtle in exchange for a promise: the day will come when the turtle will hunger to return to the place where it was shaped from the blood of the Old Ones. When you hear its voice you must act at once.' I gave her my promise. She pressed this little turtle into my hand, saying, 'Tony, you now have a sacred, secret name: Great Turtle.'"

My Hermit Uncle John was weeping. Tony turned and pressed the little stone turtle to the center of my uncle's forehead. His sobs subsided. He whispered wistfully, "I wish I could have gone up to heaven and been given a special name. Maybe I wouldn't be so afraid."

I could keep silent no longer. I burst out, "Tony, I think I *really* need to go on a vision quest."

He looked at me for a long moment before responding, "You are on one now."

"Aw, c'mon. I haven't stood in the cold on the tip of Shaman's Point and done battle with the dark star people."

A faint smile played on Tony's lips while momentarily his eyes brought his deep-running spirit in touch with mine. He explained patiently, "No two vision quests are alike as no two people are alike. No two quests need occur in the same place nor have the same shape. Your life with your daddy is your vision quest. All the powers of the dark star people are massed within him.

"You will find holy ones and be visited by spirits in many forms who will sustain you—if you let them. They will make the battle bearable, and you will discover who you really are."

I turned to my Hermit Uncle John and threw my arms around him: "You're a holy person because you help me give battle to the dark star people in my daddy."

He answered, "Maybe you've just shown me something of my name." He wept again.

I wanted Uncle John to hold me forever, but our embrace was interrupted by a sharp intake of breath from Tony. I turned to see him looking west over the lake. His right hand grasped his birth turtle. It was extended at arm's length. He seemed to be pulled off balance toward the steep drop-off which plunged downward to the water.

I watched in puzzled awe as, with difficulty, Tony pulled his arm back only to have it shoot forward once more toward the west. In hushed tones he repeated, "I will come. You will have rest."

I was frightened. "Tony, who are you talking to?"

"The heavenly turtle spirit has spoken through my birth friend. I am to return great-grandmother's gift to the blood of the Old Ones. I must go to the west at once."

He began to wrap the little worn turtle in its red cloth. All of his ritual objects were carefully stashed in his medicine bag. My Hermit Uncle John said, "I know the story. You've shared it with me before. I'll take you there."

Tony turned and looked at me. Then he stared into the west. He turned his head slightly as if listening intently. I strained my ears. The only thing I could hear were the Gunderson kids screaming swear words at one another on the next farm over.

Tony sighed and turned away as if he had just hung up some kind of spiritual telephone. He said, "The boy is to come. We will sleep now. We will awake when the Dog Star has risen and be there at sunrise."

"Be where?" I persisted.

"At the great pipestone quarries where the blood of the ancients flows. We will follow the path of my great-grandmother as we go."

I knew nothing about rising Dog Stars or blood-filled quarries, but after the activities of the afternoon I was prepared for anything.

Now, in the middle of the night, we were bouncing along from mystery to mystery.

I dozed. When I awakened, outlines of the world outside the truck were intensified in the predawn half-light. My Uncle John jabbed me gently in the ribs with his elbow saying, "W-Welcome to the l-l-land of the l-living. You were d-d-dead asleep."

Tony continued to dwell in his own space, singing the songs of his people. He was readying himself for whatever the day might bring. I was worried about the dark star people. I sure hoped they'd stay in the heavens where they belonged. Then my memory of his comments about some of them being inside my dad shocked me into full wakefulness. I wondered if there was a chance any of them were inside me—if my anger at my daddy might be made up of a whole family of dark star people.

I turned to ask Tony. His face was glowing strangely. Was it simply the light that was deepening outside? At some point during the journey he had removed the ancient turtle from his medicine bag. He held it in his hand. I stared intently at the worn little beast. Was it really creeping with infinite slowness across his palm? I wisely opted for silence.

Lights were winking on in farmhouses as we passed. Ahead, a town glowed in the lifting darkness. Our headlights flashed on a large sign: WELCOME TO PIPESTONE.

Tony's dusky voice stopped its song. He said to Uncle John, "We'll drive straight north through town. Then we'll turn slightly northwest. We're almost to the holy place."

The city was not as impressive as I had expected. There were the usual stores. Lights winked on in the rear of a restaurant. A sleepy cook was probably preparing fresh biscuits and gravy for the breakfast trade. Somehow I had expected a city sitting on the edge of mystery to have some kind of visible inner glow. As we passed out of the business district, all I saw ahead was a milkman leaving his truck to make a delivery at a still-darkened house.

We quickly returned to open country. A small sign indicated that we were approaching the Pipestone National Monument. A closed gate blocked our passage. Uncle John pulled into a nearby parking lot.

Tony continued to clutch the little turtle in his hand as he unfolded himself from his corner and stepped stiffly out of the truck. He replaced the eagle feather in his leather hat and picked up his medicine bag.

Tony stepped toward a small building, saying, "I have come here many times. I know the night watchman, Quent Four Winds. He will let us pass without my having to show papers."

My curiosity got the best of me. I asked, "What kind of papers would you have to show?"

"Anyone can visit here. Only those who are at least one fourth Native American can shape the sacred stone. Quent knows my mother was Mandan and my father Lakota. His grandfather and I were together with the Wild West Show in London."

Uncle John and I waited. We heard muffled voices. Tony returned, smiling. "I have special permission from both Quent and the Great Spirit for you both to help do what we must do."

Uncle John reached into the back of the truck and removed a small tool box. I asked him what we were going to build. He put his finger on his lips to shush me. Conversation was evidently not in order. Apparently we were about to enter some kind of church.

We stepped through the gate. I caught my breath. The light before sunrise sharply outlined every stalk of the seemingly endless flow of prairie grass. In the distance I heard waterfalls and swiftly flowing streams. Birds were awakening with lyric songs of celebration. We magically stepped into the first morning of the world.

Tony extended the little turtle before him. His arm seemed to be pulled forward by an unseen force. I wasn't surprised. He said simply, "We will follow."

We climbed a slight rise and walked across a raw granite escarpment. We stood at the edge of a cliff. Below us was a small pond fed by a waterfall. In the distance neatly kept farms stretched as far as eye could see. Near at hand was a jumble of rock formations through which a stream rambled. There were places where the granite had been chiseled away at the roots of low cliffs.

Tony said quietly, "Here the Old Ones stood."

As he reached into his medicine bag to remove the deerskin, an immediate question began to shape itself on my lips. Uncle John caught my eye and stared me into continuing silence.

Tony spread the deerskin on the edge of the cliff. He gazed to the east. The sky was aflame though the sun was not yet up.

He knelt. Uncle John and I followed suit. Tony placed the little turtle in the center of the skin. There was a sense of urgency about him as he reached for the toolbox and opened it. One by one he removed a series of about a dozen mallets, chisels, tiny saws and fine drills. He placed them in an evenly spaced circle around the bit of worn sacred stone. The little turtle looked like a small sun with the tools as its rays.

Tony removed the abalone shell, placed the herbs within it, lighted them and fanned the embers into smoke with the feather from his hat. He offered the shell to the four cardinal directions and to the sky and earth. He smudged himself, John and me in the usual manner. Chanting ancient words, he circled the smoke over the turtle and the tools as well.

The sky above us flared a deep crimson. I felt something akin to fear. I glanced behind me. I half expected mysterious red fire to explode from the rock.

Tony touched my arm. To my bewilderment he handed *me* the eagle feather and motioned for me to keep fanning the smudge in the shell.

Continuing to chant, he reached into his bag and removed his rainstick. He passed it through the smoke, offered it quickly to the six directions. He handed it to my Hermit Uncle John who moved the sacred stick in such a way that it echoed the sounds of distant water.

Tony reached into the bag a final time and removed a long object wrapped in yellow. He passed it through the smoke. From the wrapping emerged a beautiful long-stemmed pipe. The pipe bowl of the pipe was formed from the same stone as his name-object. On each side of the bowl a line of intricately carved tiny turtles held one another's tails like elephants in a circus parade.

Tony passed the pipe through the smudge. He removed a small pouch from the bag: "This is sacred tobacco, *kinnikinnik.*"

He looked at us for a moment, then held the pipe to his ear. He affirmed, "I have been granted permission to offer sacred prayers in your language so that you might become a part of the One who is all."

He took a small pinch of *kinnikinnik* and held it and the pipe stem toward the west:

> *With this wakan tobacco, I place you in the pipe,*
> *Winged Power of the west*
> *where the sun goes down.*

He placed the leaves in the pipe. Taking another pinch he turned to the north:

> *O You, Thunder-being who comes in purifying winds*
> *To guard the health of the people,*
> *I place you in the pipe,*
> *O Baldheaded Eagle of the north*
> *whose wings never tire.*

Tony's face glowed as he placed the *kinnikinnik* in the pipe. Taking another pinch, he turned to the east:

> *O sacred Long-winged Being, controller of knowledge,*
> *I place You in the pipe,*
> *You who walk the path of the rising sun,*
> *Bringing light to the world.*

The eastern sky flamed more brilliantly, but the sun did not break the horizon as Tony added the blessed tobacco. With a fourth pinch in his fingers he turned to the south:

> *O White Swan of the south where we always face,*
> *You who guard the path*

> *where our generations walk,*
> *I place you in the pipe.*

The old shaman's fingers trembled as he took a fifth pinch of the sacred herb. He turned his face to the sky. A great bird hung motionless at the zenith. Tears streamed down Tony's face as he whispered:

> *O You, Spotted Eagle, who are next to the heavens,*
> *Close to Wakan Tanka!*
> *Your wings are powerful.*
> *You are the one who takes care*
> *of the sacred circle*
> *Which surrounds us with caring.*
> *There is a place for you in the pipe.*

Doing so, he pointed the stem of the pipe to the earth. Taking another pinch of the *wakan* herb, he prayed:

> *With you we are all as relatives,*
> *Grandmother and Mother Earth who bear fruit.*
> *As I place you in the pipe,*
> *May your people walk the path of life,*
> *facing the strong winds!*
> *May we walk firmly upon you without faltering.*
> *May you strengthen our voices through this pipe*
> *As we cry to Wakan Tanka: help us!*

Turning to John and me, he whispered, "All things in the universe are in the grains of *kinnikinnik*. The whole universe is in the pipe bowl as the whole universe is in us and we are in the pipe. I send smoke as a prayer for help to *Wakan Tanka*."

Kneeling, he lighted the pipe and lifted its carved bowl to the heavens as he drew in the smoke and exhaled it. It rose upward in a thin, steady column accompanied by the stream sounds from the rainstick.

Now that the pipe was lighted, Tony rose and faced the east. As though on cue, John and I did so as well. A new chant in Lakota danced on the morning breeze with fresh vitality. Holding the pipe in both hands, Tony s-l-o-w-l-y raised it toward the heavens. As he did so, the raw orange rim of the rising sun slipped up over the horizon. I gasped. It seemed to me that the old shaman had control of the sun itself.

He stood with the pipe upraised until the entire orb had cleared the rim of trees which edged the eastern horizon. The first rays fell on the little turtle. It glowed with an inner light.

Tony sank back to the rock. Taking the pipe to his lips, he drew in the last vestiges of smoke. Continuing his ritual movements, he scattered the ashes on the wind, wrapped the pipe in its yellow cloth and returned everything to the bag and the tool chest except for the little turtle which he kept in the palm of his left hand.

He turned to me and smiled. The smile burst my interior dam and the questions flowed faster than my tongue could shape them: "Tony, wh-wh-who are the Old Ones and what were they d-doing standing up here?"

He wrapped the sacred deerskin around his shoulders and spoke: "It was long and long and long ago. Most of *Wakan Tanka's* children whom he put here on the earth were doing terrible things. They were tearing up their Mother. They were not embracing the patterns of respect for the four-leggeds and the winged ones and the finned ones. They were killing more than they needed and were not asking permission from their Mother to sustain themselves with the earth gifts.

"*Wakan Tanka* was angry. He vowed to kill all two-leggeds. He released the rivers of heaven and aimed their waters to cover the earth, killing all living things. He wanted to begin again.

"A group of Lakota loved *Wakan Tanka* and the great Earth Mother. Their lives were devoted to the sacred, yet *Wakan Tanka* in his anger had forgotten them. They gathered on this very place. They lighted the sacred fires and sprinkled them with herbs pleasant to the nostrils of the Holy One. He—"

I could stand it no longer. I burst out, "You m-m-mean the ruler of all the universe has a n-n-nose just like me and would like some of the same smells I l-like: fresh bread baking or bed sheets new dried in the spring wind?"

Uncle John was about to shush me again when Tony raised

his hand giving me permission to enter the dialogue. He responded: "*Wakan Tanka* loves the things of earth or he wouldn't have made them."

He continued, "*Wakan Tanka* took on the shape of a great white buffalo and came to the fire circle on this very spot. He made the faithful ones a promise: 'The waters will cover you, but you will live forever in a very special way. I will put your blood in a beautiful rock hidden deep beneath the granite. It will be used only to shape objects holy to me. Because your blood and spirit will be present beneath this sacred land, my children will come here when I have restored the earth and replanted people. Every tribe will be welcome—but they must dwell in peace. This must be a place of peace for all. Your spirits will speak a word of hope from your holy dwelling place in time and beyond time.'

"The waters flowed. The people perished. The blood of the Old Ones, the faithful ones, flowed into a narrow red rock band deep beneath the granite. From that day to this, those who wish to celebrate *Wakan Tanka* and Earth Mother come here and carve their objects reverently from pipestone: the blood of our ancestors."

My first impulse was to think that the whole story was dumb. But my second impulse was to sense that nobody's story is dumb. I was remembering the worst fight I'd ever seen on the school ground. Timmy McCannough had been bragging about having had something called First Communion the day before at St. Ignatius the Lesser Catholic Church. When somebody asked what that was, Timmy assured the questioner that he'd eaten some bread that had Jesus in it. Tom Suthers who went to the Baptist Church of Peter-the-Rock called him a cannibal. Timmy knocked him down, but he bounced right back up. By the time the principal separated them, both were badly battered.

That recollection helped me decide that a story about blood in a rock and a place of peace to represent that which is most holy isn't so bad after all.

I looked at Tony. He had risen. The little turtle was leading him someplace else. He had started down a steep, narrow path leading off the cliff. My Hermit Uncle John followed close on his heels, carrying the tool chest. I scrambled after them.

We descended into an area of interconnected miniature canyons through which flowed a crystal stream. Small waterfalls cascaded along the course of the stream as it meandered through this magic place. Tony paused, pointing at the granite high in front of us. It was weathered into strange shapes. He said, "Look closely. You'll see the Watcher."

There in the morning light was the profile of an Indian. As Tony turned to me, smiling, his profile almost exactly matched the ancient figure. He had stopped. His hand holding the turtle relaxed. He said softly, "Here beneath the Watcher is the place to which I have been drawn."

He again spread out the deerskin. He turned to Uncle John: "Lay out the tools. It is hard work to chip through the granite to the narrow band of sacred stone."

Uncle John and Tony each took a mallet and chisel and began to chip away the granite. I was instructed to pick up the pieces of mottled grey stone and pile them carefully to one side.

After an hour, the sun had warmed the workspace. Tony and John were sweating profusely. I knew they were going about their task all wrong. I ventured some advice: "If I'd only known w-w-what we were gonna' be d-doin' I could have been m-m-more help. I kn-know where the r-r-road workers have b-b-been storin' their d-d-dynamite. I could have g-got us a stick of dynamite and we c-could've blasted through this r-rock in n-no time!"

My Hermit Uncle John winced and looked embarrassed. Tony dropped his mallet and chisel and stared at me hard. "Didn't you listen to the story I told you on the cliff? You would tear the very heart out of Mother Earth as the ancient ones did before the flood? Boy, you must learn gentleness. It is the law of both my people and the government of this country that only simple hand tools may be used to quarry the spirit stone. With every blow of the mallet and cut of the chisel, we ask forgiveness of the Great Mother."

I was really ashamed of myself. I ventured my regrets for

my rashness: "I'm s-s-sorry, Tony. Is there s-s-some way I can apologize to M-Mother Earth?"

He handed me the mallet and chisel: "Take some strokes in the cut John and I have been making. With each blow ask her forgiveness."

I didn't really want to hit her. However, I followed my instructions. After the first couple of blows it became easier. I was pleased at my progress. The granite broke apart as I worked. Tony and Uncle John smiled.

Suddenly, a large piece of rock fell away at the back of the cut. A small opening appeared. Quickly Tony stepped forward. He reached his hand in. His face was transformed with wonder. He whispered: "It is the spot to which we have been led. My birth turtle has returned to the place from which she was carved. Look."

There at the base of the opening, illumined by a shaft of sunlight, was a band of red rock which resembled rich flowing blood. Behind it was a small cave which our quarrying had unexpectedly uncovered. Perhaps the ancient carver of the turtle had known a secret entrance and carved from the other side of the red flow.

A song of celebration rose from Tony's lips. He knelt. He prepared the smudge in the abalone shell once more and placed it in the opening.

After the cleansing he handed the shell and the feather to me. I continued to fan the smudge.

Picking up hammer and chisel, he began to outline an oval in the red rock. With each mallet blow he muttered the same phrase over and over again. It had to be his plea to Mother Earth for forgiveness.

Tony lifted out a rough-hewn piece of the red stone, passed it reverently through the smudge and laid it on the deerskin. He sprinkled a bit of sage and sweet grass in the depression from which he had taken the stone. He lifted the little worn turtle to his lips a final time. He wrapped it in its red cloth and laid it gently in the carved chamber.

He was weeping. Uncle John and I knelt on either side of him and extended supporting arms. He reached into his medicine bag and removed his eaglebone whistle. He played a lullaby.

I unsnapped the pocket of my bib overalls and took out my special friend: the teddy bear which my folks had given me when I was three on the first Christmas after they adopted me. Whenever I felt bad, I'd slip a thumb into the pocket and touch the bear. I stroked Tony's cheek with the soft fur. His eyes stopped tearing and glowed with joy as he played the final notes.

Tony and my Hermit Uncle John quickly replaced the chunks of granite they had removed. It was like watching work on a jigsaw puzzle. By the time they had finished, a casual passerby would not be able to tell the site had ever been quarried.

I thought we could pack up and leave now, but Tony had one last task. He took the piece of stone quarried from the blood of the Old Ones, held it up to the sun, stared at it intently and laid it on the deerskin.

He said, "I must do my work quickly before the stone hardens in the air." He took a tiny fine-toothed saw and made a fast rough cut. It became quickly evident that he was carving another turtle.

Sightseers had begun to pass through the area. A huge man wearing a soiled tan Stetson hat paused to watch Tony work. His worn purple shirt was stretched to its limits over his protruding belly. The center button had popped off and his navel stared out like a malevolent eye.

Spit sprayed through a large gap in his front teeth as he addressed Tony in a loud rough voice: "Hey, Big Chief! How much'll yuh take fer whatever that there thing is yer hackin' out?"

Tony stopped his work, cupping his hands over the turtle as if to protect it from the rain of spit.

He looked at the man and slowly shook his head "no."

The man pulled out a wad of bills and waved it under Tony's nose, saying, "What's the matter, Injun? Need to see the color of my money first?"

Tony continued to slowly shake his head.

The man exploded, "Well this is just about the dumbest thing I've ever seen. We feed all them helpless Injuns on the reservations, and they won't even attempt to make an honest buck."

I could stand it no longer. I shouted without a trace of a stammer, "He will never sell the blood of the Old Ones to anybody like you."

The man looked at me in disbelief saying, "Now that's just about the stupidest thing I ever heard from human lips."

He turned on his heel and started down the path. He paused, looked up and saw the Watcher carved in the rock by the wind and the rain. He picked up a stone, wound up like a crazed baseball pitcher and threw it against the ancient face. The man's raucous laugh echoed through the canyons.

He tossed out one final comment to no one in particular: "I'll bet that stone Injun is a lot smarter than the one sittin' on the ground over there."

He disappeared around a corner. I wished *Wakan Tanka* would direct a special individual flood at the offensive man and drown him.

Tony returned to his task. It was good to be alone once more.

The old shaman worked quickly. The turtle seemed to crawl out of the stone under the skill of his artistry.

When it was finished, we packed things away. Tony kept the new little turtle in his hand. He led us by a different path up onto the cliff of the Old Ones. As I expected, he again lighted the sacred fire in the abalone shell. He smudged the new turtle. He then held it to the sun for a long moment. It shone with an inner light.

He knelt by me saying, "Hold out your hand, boy."

In awe, I complied. He put the little turtle in my palm. I felt a surge of power not unlike what I'd experienced holding a stick to an electric fence. He said, "This is for you. It will guide you in whatever battles you must enter with the dark star people."

My Hermit Uncle John whispered softly, "I'm real proud of you, Rog. I think you've just been chosen for something special."

That was scary. I guessed that the combat would be long and sometimes painful. I nestled the little turtle in the side pocket of my overalls.

Without further ado, Tony led us quickly to the truck. It was only mid-morning. The purpose for our trip had been accomplished. He seemed eager to return to Lake Sumach.

We kept to the main roads this time. My Hermit Uncle John dropped me at the end of our farm driveway. I thanked Tony for the special gift, said my good-byes, and walked slowly down the lane, stroking the turtle in my pocket. Now my bear would have a helpful friend in the sometimes overwhelming task of comforting me.

In the gathering dusk, I headed for the barn. Dad seemed glad to see me. He didn't question me about my absence. He commented that he hoped I'd thank my mom for milking my cows that morning. We set about the tasks leading up to the evening struggle with Old Dora and the rest of the herd of milk cows.

It was two weeks later when my father began another battle with the dark star people. He'd asked me to bring a can of gasoline to fill the tractor. The can was heavy. I tripped over a wagon tongue and went sprawling. Only a little gas spilled. It took only a small misdemeanor on my part to bring down his wrath.

The air was filled with the usual barrage of invectives centering on my general worthlessness. My hand slipped into my pocket to stroke the holy turtle. It reminded me that I was a person of infinite worth. I was good.

I held my head a little higher in the face of the onslaught. The fact that I didn't cringe only angered him more. He noticed the outline of my hand in my pocket.

He exploded: "What the hell are you doing in your pocket? Playing with yourself while I'm trying to talk some sense into you?"

He grabbed my hand from my pocket. The turtle flew out

of my fingers and fell at his feet. I stood in stark terror as he bent over and picked it up. He examined it clinically.

He said with feigned quietness, "Well, ain't this somethin', though. My son carries around a funny–shaped hunk of rock to distract his poor self while his daddy tries to talk some common, practical sense into him. Well, we'll see about this. You jist come for a little walk with me, boy."

He led me into the shop attached to the garage. There was a small forge with an anvil at its side and an assortment of steel mallets. He put the little turtle on the anvil and picked up a large mallet. He slammed down the great hammer. A single blow pulverized the soft stone into fine dust.

He did not stop with one strike. He slammed down the mallet again and again and again. Sweat poured from him. With each blow my remaining respect for him diminished.

He threw down the mallet and stepped toward me. He was breathing heavily from his exertion. He stood in front of me for a moment and then slapped me hard. From long, harsh experience I fell to the floor to avoid a second blow.

He turned to leave the shop. He paused and flung a final threat at me: "If you ever again bring a damn fool thing like that onto this property, I'll give you something to really remember who's in charge around here."

I rose and stumbled to the anvil. It was covered with red dust as fine as talcum. I thought for a moment and then slipped to the door. My father was nowhere in sight. I crept down the path to the two-seater outhouse. I knew there was an outdated Sears Roebuck catalogue which we used in place of toilet tissue. In the back was an envelope for mailing in order blanks.

I tore it out and slipped back into the shop. With as much care as possible, I brushed the fine powder into the envelope. I also brushed the head of the mallet. I wanted to lose as little of the blood of the Old Ones as possible.

I carefully placed the envelope in the pocket of my bib overalls next to the bear and walked into the house. My dad was sitting in his old oak rocking chair with his head in his hands.

The dark star people possessed him. He sat exhausted from their twisting of his spirit. I choked back sobs. I knew that somewhere within him was a daddy who could laugh and hold me and dry my tears with his big red and white polkadotted handkerchief. Would he ever escape and come back to me again?

I told my mom I wasn't hungry—that I was heading to my Hermit Uncle John's after I finished the milking. She saw my bruised face and kissed it lightly.

The full moon lighted my way. Ahead, I saw outlined against it a familiar figure. No one else that I knew wore a leather hat with an eagle feather.

My tears began to flow. I ran across the field to meet him. I entered his extended arms and sobbed out the fate of the sacred turtle. I reached into my pocket and handed him the envelope.

Without a word, he opened it. Three times he moistened his finger in my tears, dipped it in the fine red dust and stroked a pattern on my left cheek.

He resealed the envelope and slipped it into his medicine bag. He hugged me again and went on his wordless way.

I went back home. On the kitchen table was a note: "I'm taking some soup to Mrs. Killian. She's near death again."

Unable to do anything for my father and abandoned by me, Mom could at least take care of the rest of the world.

Dad was still sitting silently in his chair, his head in his hands. The tin water cup on the nail keg table at his elbow was empty. Tony had touched me tenderly. Maybe I could even do something for my daddy.

I stepped to the kitchen, filled the cup from the bucket and returned to the living room. I was about to set it on the keg when Dad threw his head back against the chair and opened his eyes. I held the cup to his lips. He drank deeply. A faint smile played on his lips for a moment. He fell into an untroubled sleep.

I slipped into my room. I lighted the kerosene lamp on my bureau. I looked into the cracked mirror. On my left cheek was a small turtle outlined in the blood of the Old Ones.

INTERLUDE 3

The grandfather clock tolled seven. Tony awoke from a fitful sleep and sat bolt upright, crying out with great agitation, "The show! I'm going to be late for the show! Colonel Cody will be furious. I carry the flag in the opening parade."

He was gasping for breath. I gentled him and assured him that he was safe in bed at John Robbennolt's. He looked around wildly, then focused on me and breathed out, "Rog."

His hands wandered aimlessly over the bedding. I climbed up and turned the lamp wick down a bit so the room was not quite so light.

His scattered words gathered themselves into that familiar litany:

O Cody!
Longhair Bill Cody!
How many times must you kill my people?
How many times must you kill my heart?

Food was always delayed in coming to the reservation...boredom came early...we were captive animals...looked on as helpless children...cheated ever by the agents...swept by sickness...no freedom to kill the food we needed...the government ordered wanton killing of the buffalo to force us to the reservations...we were urged to become simple plowmen...urged to worship the wasichu God and his son Jesus...while the wasichu God-worshipers cheated our people, stole our holy lands. Hetchetu welo!

Word came that Cody, great Indian scout for the bluecoated slayers, had become great Indian friend...someone had a newspaper from Canada with Cody's picture and good-sounding words...I read them again and again, trying to erase the picture of the man on Tall Bull's great horse leading our people to slavery..."In nine cases out of ten when there is trouble between white men and Indians, it will be found that the white man is responsible. Indians expect a man to keep his word. They can't understand how a man can lie. Most of them would as soon cut off a leg as tell a lie."

It was soon said on our reservation at Pine Ridge that Cody needed Indians to act in his great show...that he would take them to New York to Madison Square Garden...I signed an agreement for twenty-five dollars a month...I saw the show as my pathway to freedom...but the contract was written so that the Show kept forty percent of all we earned to be paid to us only when we returned to captivity...I signed the contract...rode the railroad the first time...played before thousands of people who came to see the Wild West "as it really was, as we really were."

Each night I rode wildly...reenacting the Summit Springs Battle where Tall Bull was killed...I held the white actress, threatening her death until rescued by Cody...I attacked an immigrant wagon train crossing the plains until repulsed by scouts and cowboys led by Cody...I attempted an ambush of a Pony Express Rider in the form of Bill Cody...I did war dances and games with the hundred show Indians...I attacked the Deadwood Mail coach until it was saved by Cody and cowboys...I herded eighteen buffalo around the stage, remembering my starving people, while we demonstrated how Indians killed them and Cody displayed his hunting techniques...I attacked a settler's cabin until it was rescued by Cody, frontiersmen, cowboys and scouts.

Night after night that's how thousands saw us: as attackers and rapists and murderers and thieves in this "true representation of the American West"...we were Cody's "children," he treated us well...but I could not forget that night in the mountains when my brother was born...I could not blot out the multitude's cheers as we were defeated night after night in the show, as we had been in real life.

I said to Bill Cody one day in rehearsal, "Can we have just one time when the Indians win?"...Cody looked flustered, "The crowd wouldn't like it"...he turned on his heel and walked quickly away...later he added "Custer's Last Stand"...as the

Indians triumphed, the audience booed...Cody rode into the center of the carnage and whispered "Too late"...as if the outcome would have been different had he been there.

Over the years, I'm haunted by memories...the looks of derision on the faces of people...the screams of glee when six times a night I was shot from my horse and groveled in the dirt...we were not perfect people...we struggled for the right path...but there was something of beauty in life as we lived it...there was something of beauty in life as we lived it...there was something of beauty in life as we lived it...Hetchetu welo!

His voice trailed off. I thought the old man was asleep. But his lips still moved. I placed my ear close to them. He was repeating over and over again:

O Cody!
Longhair Bill Cody!
Generations have passed
And I must forgive you.

After a few moments, his breathing eased. He slept.

RESURRECTION

Lightning tore the midnight sky. My battered body felt energy flowing from the jagged shafts of fire. I was running away from darkness in the dark. I had stumbled across the fields so many times I needed no light to guide me.

As my screaming daddy stood over me earlier in the evening, I was sure I would never see the sunrise again. It was the Saturday before Easter. I thought we'd been having a perfect day together. Mom always liked to color a few eggs to celebrate the holy season.

Dad thought it would be good if we made some homemade ice cream. He even kidded me a bit as I knelt turning the handle on the freezer: "Hey, boy. When yuh turn yer head jist right in the sunshine, I think I spot a little fuzz comin' on yer face. I'm goin' to have to teach you to shave one of these days. You probably also got a little fuzz comin' a coupla' places lower down. Yuh may git to be a man yet."

I blushed with pleasure.

An hour later he came up from the shop where I heard him sharpening a plowshare. His face was a blank mask. He passed me without acknowledging my presence.

Five hours later he was beating me with the curved end of his sheepherder's crook. Each blow called forth the pain of every blow he'd inflicted on me in the past. The joints in my body hurt as I thought about moving after this moment in hell was over. I wondered if the day would come when all that was left of me would somehow explode as the terror reached its climax.

Now, I tripped over a root and fell face downward on the soft earth of a new-plowed field. The lightning flashed again. Lifting my head, I saw Troy Pedersen's straw stack. His cows had eaten a kind of cave in its side. During last summer's early August heat I had enlarged the opening as a momentary place of refuge from the merciless sun while I shocked oats for Troy. Maybe I could make it there and simply collapse for the night.

A soft rain began to fall. The shock of its coolness revived me enough to crawl toward the haven ahead. I shivered. Another kind of lightning tore through my system. The white heat of pain intensified with every shake.

I reached my destination. I crawled into the den of straw. My nose immediately informed me that I was not alone. The little grotto smelled like the air outside the Dew Drop Inn on a hot summer night. All the incense from the booze being consumed inside by the crowd of men sprinkled with a few "bold" women would float outside, partially carried by the patrons as they moved uncertainly toward home.

My ears completed the identification of the one who had taken up residence in my special place. A chant rose above heaven's thunder. I had heard that sound many times. Its lilt had often carried me into another world beyond the darkness of life with my sick father. Now it was garbled, intermittent.

A moment of light illumined Tony Great Turtle. He was curled into a tight ball, his head on his medicine bag. Everything my daddy had told me about Indians swept across my mind: "Indians are a filthy, flea-ridden lot of drunken killers. Don't you ever have nothin' to do with 'em."

I had asked, "D-D-Dad, did you ever have anything t-t-to do with an Indian d-directly?"

He looked at me in disgust at my stupidity for even asking such a question: "Of course I have. Jist yesterday, Perfessor Grisham's Traveling Herbal Emporium set up in the lot next to the sign of the flying red horse at the gas station. Every year when he comes I git myself at least two bottles of his world-famous foolproof headache elixir.

"Well, I didn't know he'd come, and I ended up in town on a Friday night with only enough cash fer a few groceries. I had jist turned the corner by the Dew Drop Inn when I ran right square into this old Indian. I asked him what the hell he was doin' standin' in my way.

"He said he had a favor to ask of me. Well, I wasn't about to do no favors for no Indian. Then, he pulled out a wad of bills and asked me if I'd go into the liquor store by the Dew Drop Inn and buy him a quart of whiskey. He'd give me two bucks extry to do it.

"Well, I sure didn't want to put no drunken Indian on the streets of Pheasant Valley. On the other hand, since there was some kinda' law sayin' Indians couldn't buy booze on their own and take it out of the store, somebody else'd buy his booze and I might as well make the profit. Besides, the elixir was a buck a bottle so I'd come out real good.

"I took his money, bought the likker and stepped back outside. I found him sort of hunched over on the street corner. He'd taken off his leather hat with the big feather in it and was fanning himself. I gave him the whiskey and his change which I counted out real careful-like so's he couldn't never say I'd cheated him. He handed me two worn one dollar bills and turned and walked off into the dark.

"He didn't even thank me fer what I'd done fer him, so I called out, 'Hey! Big Chief! Don't they teach yuh to say thank you on the reservation?' I jist thought I'd give him a little lesson in manners. I didn't git a word back from him.

"Well, I got to talkin' to some of the neighbors about the terrible drought, and it was late before I got up to the Perfessor's. There was a crowd standin' around. Some of them were buyin'. Some were just admirin' the beautiful team of black horses the Perfessor used to pull his gilded caravan around the country.

"I got into line. Folks'd tell the Perfessor jist what was

ailin' 'em and he'd prescribe something special fer each one of 'em from about sixty different flasks and bottles and boxes he had on display. When I got to the front of the line, he recognized me.

"He said real loud so's everybody 'round could hear, 'Well, if it isn't the man with the world's biggest headache. Good people, this is one of my best, most regular customers. Every year when I visit your fair city, he buys a twelve month supply of my miracle headache elixir.'

"He added, 'We've just sold the last bottle, but my assistant, a renowned Sioux medicine man, is just now bottling our secret mixture of herbs and water from a healing spring blessed by an appearance of the Virgin Mary herself.

"'So sir, you finish your shopping and come back in half an hour. Just make sure if you spend any time in the Dew Drop Inn you save a dollar and one thin dime for each bottle.'

"He got a real good laugh from the crowd at that one, and then he continued, 'When you return, not only will you be blessed by bottles of my world-renowned cure, but my assistant will demonstrate some dances made famous by the savages of the plains.'"

My father continued, "I was a little miffed. The Perfessor had raised his prices a dime a bottle since last year. I left and circled 'round behind the caravan. To my surprise, there was the same old Indian, nekkid to the waist, squattin' on the ground. He was filling fancy brown bottles with green liquid from a battered tub. The bottle of whiskey was open at his side. It was about half empty. His hand was shakin' so that the elixir kept runnin' down his bare arm back into the tub.

"I walked over to him and said, 'Hey, Big Chief, looks like yer havin' yerself a party all alone back here. Listen, I didja' a favor a little while back. Now I'd like yuh to do one fer me. Why don'tcha jist hand me a coupla' bottles of that there medicine yuh got already corked up. I'll give yuh back yer two bucks and we'll be even.

"He stared at me fer a minute and then handed me two

bottles. I draped the dollar bills over the open top of the whiskey and left.

"I went to the Red Owl store an' bought a few groceries. I walked past the lot on the way back to the truck. I stayed in the shadows so the Perfessor wouldn't see me. There was a big crowd watchin' the old Indian dancin' under the street light. He beat a little drum real slow like, and he was hoppin' first on one foot an' then on the other. He was starin' at the moon. All of a sudden he lost his balance and fell flat on his face in the dirt. The crowd roared.

"The Perfessor started his spiel and everybody turned around and forgot about the old Indian in the dirt.

"I got into my truck. I'd been feelin' a headache a'comin' on all day so I uncorked one of the bottles and took a good swig. Then I headed off fer home. I got a coupla' miles outside of town and all of a sudden I was so sick to my stomach I couldn't stand it. I stopped the truck, jumped out and threw up in the ditch so bad I thought my insides were comin' outside.

"Somethin' was wrong with the elixir. The drunken Indian probably had made a mistake in the mixin'. Maybe the crazy old coot had spit in it or somethin'. I do have to admit by the time I got home I didn't have no headache no more.

"And so kid, this all goes to show yuh that yer daddy knows quite a bit about Indians, and one of the things I know fer sure is that yuh can't trust a one of 'em."

I remembered my Hermit Uncle John saying that the first time Tony appeared at the sacred site on the lakeshore he had come from dancing in a medicine show. The Indian of my daddy's story certainly was Tony. For the first time that long night of terror I wept. Maybe my daddy was right.

The storm passed. The man in the full moon stared coldly at the curled figure lying with his head on his leather bag. I crouched on the opposite side of the straw cave.

The chant choked off. The old man's body gave a long shudder. He stumbled to his feet, lurched outside and retched.

He turned and spotted me sobbing in the corner. His body

straightened. Sobered by the sight, he moved slowly toward me. He knelt down and reached a hand toward my shoulder. I slapped it away. I shouted at him, "G-Get away from m-m-me. All that stuff about b-being in t-t-t-touch with *Wakan Tanka* is a c-crock. You're j-j-just another d-dirty old drunken Indian that c-can't be t-trusted."

He sank to the ground. He whispered, "Battles with the dark star people come in many ways. For me now they live in a bottle. They draw me to them with the promise that I will be able to forget—forget the starvation, and the broken promises, and the reservation, and the laughter at the Wild West Show when we were forced to do our most sacred acts, and the terror I have caused in many ways you don't know about. I drink them in and remember only more intently. Beneath the memories I hear their wild laughter of triumph."

"Oh, Tony, w-what are we going to do? Is there any way that we can k-k-keep the dark star people away from y-you and my d-d-daddy. I don't think I can st-stand any more disappointment."

Wearily he rose to his feet and reached a hand to me. I hesitated. Then I allowed my hand to find its way into his familiar one. He said, "It's just past midnight. There's time. We'll go to the shore of Lake Sumach and see if we can build a healing fortress against the dark star people."

He picked up his medicine bag, and we moved off through the night. The eye of the man in the moon followed us, curious to see what this strange pair of two-leggeds was going to do. I looked back at the cave. An edge of moonlight glittered on the partially empty bottle standing within easy reach of the depression made by the old man's tortured body.

We arrived on the high bank of the holy lake. Stars were criss-crossed by flights of silent night birds. Tony laid his bag on the launching rock, put his hat atop it and began unbuttoning his denim jacket. I looked at him quizzically and asked, "W-What are we g-g-going to d-d-do, Tony?" My disappointment at his drunkenness brought back my stammer even in his presence.

He paused for a moment and spread his arms to the heavens, saying, "It is late in the Moon of the Red Grass Appearing (April). It is a time for cleansing."

I blurted out, "T-Tony, are you t-t-trying to t-trick *Wakan T-Tanka* into forgetting that I f-found you d-d-dead d-drunk in a st-st-straw stack?"

He drew in a sharp breath and whispered, "*Wakan Tanka* is not to be tricked. We are to be forgiven."

I exploded, "I ain't done n-nothing wr-wrong. It's my d-d-daddy who b-beat me so b-b-bad that every j-j-joint hurts when I m-m-move."

He swung around to me, dropped on one knee and took my shoulders in the firm grasp of his big hands. His eyes were two pits of moon-ignited fire. He said softly, deliberately, "I worked awhile for a traveling lady preacher. I set up her tent and her chairs. She was real good to me. Every night folks would pack her services. Most of the time they were more curious to hear a woman preach than to have their souls saved, but there were times when even that seemed to happen. Every night Miss Helen would repeat three or four times, 'All have sinned and come short of the glory of God.'

"When my great-grandmother taught me to be a carrier of the holy ways, she said the most important patterns of all were those which cleansed and brought forgiveness. You'll never be whole as long as you hate your sick daddy. We both need cleaning up and forgiving. Now do as I tell you and take your clothes off."

I'd heard Pastor Pfitz at the Baptist Church of Peter-the-Rock use those same words about everybody sinning. A picture squirreled up out of my imagination: the pastor invited everybody in the congregation to save their sinful selves by throwing their clothes off and marching together into the lake, singing "Onward, Christian Soldiers." I imagined what some of those folk might look like without any clothes on: Felicty Evans with her pendulous breasts and Cleota Collins who always kept hers hidden behind tightly folded arms and Dink Tomlinson who was always massaging his groin as he stood in the barn talking to my dad and skinny Graciella Greardon and tubby old Wally Mertwuller.

I was shaken by uncontrollable giggles. As Tony removed his worn denim jacket, he turned and silenced me with a stare. I fumbled with the buckles on my overalls. I finally got the straps down from my shoulders, slipped out of my ragged shirt and dropped the shorts my ma had made from a flour sack. I was told I had to start wearing something under my overalls because I was "gettin' big."

The night breeze was cold. I shivered and the pain returned. Tony had taught me the Lakota names for the months. While he removed his heavy shoes I ventured a proposition, "Tony, I-I-I'm freezin' out here. I-I-I think I'd rather w-w-wait until the Moon when the Cherries Turn Black (August) to be cleaned up and f-f-forgiven."

He said simply, "*Wakan Tanka* will warm the water."

That was a scary thought. We'd just read a story in school about a dragon who lived in a lake. When he crawled out he could vaporize a village with a single blast of fire from his nostrils. If that was going to be how *Wakan Tanka* warmed the lake, I wanted no part of it.

Tony grasped me by the hand and led me to the edge of the water. I made one last attempt to delay entering the frigid lake: "T-T-Tony, don't we have to do some other st-stuff before we g-g-go into the water, like b-b-burn some s-sage or something?"

He smiled down at me. He bent over with cupped hands and dipped up some water. A motion of his head indicated I was to do the same. I followed his every move. We offered the water to the four directions as Tony chanted. Some of the water ran down my bare arm. *Wakan Tanka* was being a bit tardy in following through on his responsibilities to warm the water. I really wished we'd waited until the Moon when the Cherries Turn Black.

He held the water in his cupped hands over the ground on the lakeshore. His song rose. The lake breeze quieted. In the incredible stillness it seemed as if all creation were waiting for something special to happen. I didn't know what he was saying, but it felt as if my very soul were being drawn out of my body and into the night sky.

He let the water stream into Mother Earth. My hands containing the icy liquid seemed frozen together. My teeth were chattering. I said, "Tony, is th-th-there something I should s-say to M-M-Mother Earth in my language?"

He spoke a line and paused, and I repeated:

> This water is from the four parts of the universe,
> It will be returned by the power of Father Sky.
> Mother Earth has gifted us with water,
> By thanking her with this gift,
> She will empower us to walk through troubles.

I let the water trickle into the sand on the shore of the holy lake.

Tony took my hand again. We walked across the great flat rock from which ancient canoes had been launched. Tony knew a path where our bare feet would not be cut by the granite ridges.

The rock sloped down into the water. I experienced a moment of terror since I did not know how to swim. The moon was hanging behind the cross on the Baptist Church of Peter-the-Rock. Its light glowed in a path on the surface of the perfectly still water. It looked like we could walk on the light path straight up to the steepled cross. Wouldn't the worshipers be surprised when they arrived for the Easter sunrise service and found an old Indian and a boy in their birthday suits sitting on the arms of the cross?

The distraction in my grasshopper mind was fortunate. It lessened the initial shuddering shock. We had walked further into the holy lake. Every part of my body seemed to shrink defensively in upon itself. The pain from my earlier beating shrank as well.

We waded out to our armpits. Tony's song rose heavenward. He put his hand on my head and gently shoved me beneath the surface as he lowered his face and shoulders under the water.

As we came up, the western sky was tattooed with a meteor

shower. Warmth flooded my body. Within Tony and me a few more dark star people had been defeated.

We followed the trail of light back to the shore. I walked toward my clothes. I would dry myself with my shirt, leave it off and find someplace to curl up and sleep. That was not to be. Tony reached into his leather bag and pulled out his sacred deerskin. He wrapped it around his waist. He said, "Put on your shorts. We'll prepare the Holy of Holies." I picked up the crudely stitched underwear. We always bought Robin Hood Flour. The picture of the storied hero shooting an arrow was stretched across the seat. As I pulled them up, I wondered in passing if Robin Hood and his merry men could have joined up with the Lakota, maybe they would have been able to kill off enough *wasichus* to save their sacred Black Hills.

Then I remembered that I, too, was a *wasichu*. However, at the moment I didn't feel much like one. I felt like somebody who was more at home on moon paths in star lands.

Tony picked up his bag and headed toward a stand of willows just to the east of us. I'd noticed a few days before that they were in full new leaf. It looked to me as if the lights of heaven were fading a bit in that direction.

Tony stopped at a hole around which were charred bits of wood. I wondered if some fisher folk had paused here for a wiener roast. The thought reminded me that it had been a l-o-n-g time since I had eaten.

There was a stack of wood nearby with a canvas tarp over it to keep it dry. Tony said, "You have been cold. We will light a sacred fire, the *Peta-owihankeshni*, the 'Fire of no end.'"

I was glad. I brought him an armload of wood. I was about to simply throw it into the hole when he stopped me saying, "There must always be a pattern. There must always be gentleness. Watch carefully. I place four pieces running east and west and four pieces running north and south so that the four directions are honored. Then we make a tepee of sticks beginning with the west and moving to the north, east and south."

He nodded to a nearby pile of rocks: "Bring me four of them."

I knew exactly what I was to do and placed them gently in the four directions in the right order. Tony chanted in Lakota and then for my benefit sang:

> O *Wakan Tanka,*
> *We place these rocks at the four quarters,*
> *We understand You are at the center.*
> *Sacred rocks, help us to do the will of Grandfather.*

He motioned for more stones. I protested: "Tony, this is getting to be hard work. Why don't you just tell me a story about what it is you intend to do?"

Tony turned and gave me a penetrating look. When he spoke, there was fire in his eye: "My great-grandmother said to me once when I was a boy making comments like yours, 'If I tell you, you'll forget. If I show you, you may not remember. If I make you an active part of it all, you'll understand.' That's the reason for everything we do in our ceremonies. No one can simply listen or look on. They will lose touch with the *wakan* at the heart of all. Now act. Bring the rocks."

I brought the rocks. I mounded them over the wood. He removed a match from his bag. He gathered some twigs and put them against the wood on the east. He lighted the fire. The wood caught quickly. A chant flowed in Lakota and English. I knew that we were to be healed somehow by the light of the eternal fire which was the sun and *Wakan Tanka* and a whole lot of other things. I knew that the whole universe was somehow being put together before my very eyes.

Tony took the canvas from the woodpile. On the ground was a set of deer antlers, a tin pail and a branch of sage. Nestled in the wood was a tin box. From the box he removed a sharp knife, a ball of twine and a little hatchet.

He handed me the knife. Taking the hatchet, he approached the willow. His chant rose to a wail as he lifted the hatchet and cut off a heavy branch. He handed it to me. I didn't have to be told what to do. I stripped off the leaves. With each slash of the knife I whispered, "Forgive me, forgive me, forgive me."

Tony cut sixteen branches. He took the knife and cut lengths of twine. He paced off ten steps east from the fire. There was another indentation in the earth. It was perfectly round. He motioned that the branches were to be bowed over the central pit. We each took the end of a branch and shoved its ends into the soft earth. Tony tied a bit of twine around each of the joints where the branches met.

Soon we had a beautiful little round lodge framed up. Tony removed his bag of sage and sprinkled some over the ground inside. We picked up the canvas and gently laid it over the frame. It fit exactly. An entry flap faced to the east. I knew for certain that what I was doing had been done many times before.

He said, "Go fetch John. He is a most holy man. He will help us with our final purification in our *inipi*, our sweat lodge."

I had always figured that my Hermit Uncle John was special. I didn't even protest the idea of awakening him so early in the morning.

I stepped into his shack. His little dog, Tiny, didn't even bark but merely stretched and licked my hand. I stepped to John's bed. The moonlight poured through the window. Despite the terror he'd experienced in the War to End All Wars, his face was incredibly peaceful. I touched his shoulder. His eyes shot open. Seeing me standing there in my underwear, he grinned and said, "Tony's with you, isn't he? From the looks of things, by morning you'll know a bit more about what it means to be a man."

He pulled on his clothes. The great clock struck four.
He paused and picked up a small drum from a table in front of the thunderbird outlined in arrowheads on a wall mat.

When we arrived at the *inipi*, Tony was standing looking out over the lake. He said, "My people have been doing these most sacred acts on this very spot for hundreds and hundreds of years. They have come and gone but always returned. Any hope I have to remain in touch with the Old Ones and the Holy One lies here."

Uncle John placed the drum by the entry flap of the little lodge. He picked up the pail and headed for the lake. Tony and

I went through the ceremony of blessing and filling his pipe as we'd done at the pipestone quarries. Tony leaned it against a stone near the pit where the rocks were beginning to glow with heat. He took off his deerskin and knelt at the entrance. He motioned me to follow. I slipped out of my shorts and crawled into the little lodge. Outside there had been the glow of the fire and the dull light of the heating rocks. Now there was only deep darkness as Tony closed the entry flap.

I panicked. I reached out a hand. I could not find my companion and guide. Had he been spirited away into Mother Earth's womb? I felt for a moment that I was in the mouth of a gigantic beast whose razor sharp teeth were about to slash me senseless.

Then I heard his voice repeating, *"hee-ay-hay-ee-ee"* in patterns of fours. He paused and whispered, "Sing the ancient song with me. It is sung when our hearts are heavy with darkness and we hunger for light."

Together we sang the song.

It must have been a familiar cue. The tent flap opened. Uncle John knelt there, extending the pipe to Tony. He quickly returned with a glowing rock balanced on the antlers. Our nostrils were assailed by the acrid smell of the hot rock on the bare horn. He extended his arms into the lodge and dropped the rock into the center of the fire pit. Tony explained, "This rock is for *Wakan Tanka* who is the center of all."

My mind flipped back to the Gospel story which my Hermit Uncle John had read to me on the Friday strangely labeled "Good." After Jesus had been killed on the cross, they put his body in a cave and rolled a stone in front of it. That stone was sort of the center of the universe. It was as if they had put Jesus in some kind of sweat lodge with God rolled across the entrance.

My reverie was interrupted by John placing rocks in the four directions, an additional one for the earth, and some final rocks mounded in the center. Tony touched each rock with the foot of the pipe and intoned its purpose now completely in English. It finally dawned on me that all the ceremonies were variations on centeredness.

Uncle John set the pail of water and the sage branch inside the lodge and closed the flap. In a moment he began to tap out a rhythm on the little drum.

Sparks shot from the heated rocks. It felt like we were lost deep in galactic darkness amongst the farthest stars. Multiple sparks hovered for a moment like miniature constellations and then fell back to the pit like defeated dark star people. With each fall I somehow felt lighter.

Tony sang to John's beat:

Fire, most powerful of all things,
Great gift of Wakan Tanka,
You are set in the place of honor at our center.
May you always be our center within us and without.
Help us in what we are about to do
That we may be forgiven and gifted with new life.

Tony took the branch of sage and sprinkled water from the holy lake five times over the heated rocks, intoning:

Water of life, I offer you
Once for our Grandfather, Tunkashila,
Once for our Father, Ate,
Once for our Grandmother, Unchi,
Once for our Mother, Ina, the Earth
And once for the sacred pipe.

In the blood-red light from the glowing rocks I watched him light the pipe. After the ritual blessing he handed it to me. I inhaled a bit of the mild sweet smoke from the *kinnikinnik*. My sense of floating deepened.

A wild cry escaped the old shaman. I had to piece together his muddled outpouring of Lakota and English:

O Wakan Tanka, look at us within the Sacred Hoop.
We are all people.
As we offer ourselves to you,
We offer all people to you
That we may somehow live together.
We wish to live again!

Another cry of anguish rose from the sweat lodge as he

sobbed out, "Help Us!"

The hot steam quickly filled the tiny enclosed space redolent with the smell of sage and sweet grass. Sweat poured from me. The pain from my father's beating flowed out as well. It was as if my very body was dissolving, leaving whatever was really me hovering.

I sensed a gigantic wing stretching over me to keep me from floating away. At the same time, a rock cracked and a bolt of sparks shaped a zigzag red line forked at each end.

Tears flowed. The fire sign was that of *Wakinyan-Tanka*, the great Thunderbird. He had come to save me from my fear, to keep me suspended between his jet-black feathers and Mother Earth.

Time stopped. I spun in this all-in-all world like a lonely planet.

I was shocked into a sense of real space by the touch of Tony's hand upon my head. He was massaging water into my hair. He said softly, "Dip your hands into the water and rub it over your entire body."

I did as I was told. He reached over and rubbed water softly down my back. I did the same for him. He raised the bucket a final time to the four directions and drained it onto the hot rocks. A final burst of steam momentarily took my breath away.

Tony sang:

> We have made ourselves pure and white as new snow;
>   We are in darkness, but light will soon come.
> When we leave this lodge,
>   May we be safe from the dark star people.
> As we leave behind all impure thoughts and
>   ignorant acts,
> May we be as children newly born!
> May we live again, O Wakan Tanka.

Uncle John opened the lodge flap. Red bands of light leaped against the intense gold of the eastern sky, as if the glow of the rocks had been carried by the Thunderbird into the heavens and lavishly expanded across the retreating darkness.

The morning star was waning. Pausing at the entrance, Tony intoned:

O Morning Star, you lead the dawn as it walks forth
And also the day which follows with its Light
which is wisdom.
May we not return to the paths of evil
As we emerge newborn to walk the earth.

I sensed a note of desperation in his voice. I remembered the bottle glinting in the moonlit straw cave.

In the center of the path leading to the heating pit for the sacred stones John had placed a final rock fresh from the dying fire. He sprinkled sage on it and fanned it with the feather from the old man's hat. Tony rose slowly from where he knelt at the entrance to the little lodge. He faltered, swaying for a moment in the now-strange world into which we were emerging. He seemed steadied by unseen hands. Had the "friends" from Shaman's Point come to his aid?

He resolutely walked through the smoke from the rock. I followed. He spoke final ritual words:

*This is the fragrance of **Wakan Tanka**.*
Through this the two-leggeds, the four-leggeds,
the winged ones,
And all the peoples of the universe will be happy
and will rejoice!
*It is finished! **Hetchetu alo!***

John disappeared into his rough cabin. Tony was walking toward the holy lake. I followed him. My feet barely brushed the earth.

We walked into the mirror-like lake a second time on that strange journey. For the first time in my life, I was unafraid of the water. When we were shoulder-deep, we once again lowered our heads beneath the surface. As we emerged from the water the sun burst its eastern bonds. The empty cross on the Baptist Church of Peter-the-Rock flared in triumph.

The congregation gathered on the far bank lifted their voices in "Christ the Lord is Risen Today" interspersed with alleluias:

Lives again our glorious king
Where, O death, is now thy sting?
Dying once he all doth save,
Where thy victory, O grave?
Soar we now where Christ has led,
Following our exalted Head,
Made like him, like him we rise,
Ours the cross, the grave, the skies;
Hail the Lord of earth and heaven!
Praise to thee by both be given,
Thee we greet triumphant now,
Hail, the Resurrection thou!

As Tony and I half floated, half walked out of the sacred depths, his face was radiant. The sun reflecting from water drops cast an aura around his naked body. I knew I was following a brother of the risen Lord. But was he not my brother as well?

Tony put an arm around me and drew me close. He said softly, "Something came alive in both of us this morning. My lost wholeness returned for awhile. New strength rose up in you."

I responded, "Tony, you won't really need the whiskey anymore, will you?"

After a long moment, he said slowly, "It's never been a question of need. It's always been a matter of letting things uncenter me so bad that I wander beyond the Sacred Hoop. We always need ways of drawing back or being drawn back or being led back."

Well, I thought, that's Tony's journey. There were some pretty uncentering things awaiting me. I had experienced the resurrection of hope. How could I stay in touch with it and not let my response to my daddy's "touch" destroy it?

As we neared the rock, we saw a figure standing there. I blinked my eyes. It looked like the Christ from the stained-glass window. I blinked again. John was walking toward us. He handed each of us a towel. We dried ourselves, slipped on our clothes and followed the old hermit into his shack.

The table was set for three. On a fourth chair sat Pity Me, the skunk, meticulously washing her paws.

From the kitchen came the homey incense of frying bacon. A bowl of pancake batter and some eggs stood in readiness. Tony and I watched as my Hermit Uncle John broke three eggs on the cast-iron griddle and quickly surrounded each of them with the rich batter. I was delighted. We were going to have "Sun on the Mountain" for Easter breakfast.

Tony and I were extra hungry after our spirited journey. We each had three helpings. As we slowly finished our final round, Uncle John reached for his Bible. He began to read a different version of the Easter story from the one read two days ago. This was from the Gospel of Mark:

> And when the sabbath was past, Mary Magdalene, and Mary the mother of James, and Salome had bought sweet spices, that they might come and anoint him. And very early in the morning, the first day of the week, they came unto the sepulchre at the rising of the sun.
>
> And they said among themselves, "Who shall roll us away the stone from the door of the sepulchre?" And when they looked, they saw that the stone was rolled away: for it was very great.
>
> And entering into the sepulchre, they saw a young man sitting on the right side, clothed in a long white garment; and they were affrighted. And he saith unto them, "Be not affrighted: ye seek Jesus of Nazareth, which was crucified: he is risen; he is not here: behold the place where they laid him. But go your way, tell his disciples and Peter that he goeth before you into Galilee: there shall ye see him, as he said unto you."

My Hermit Uncle John paused. No one spoke for a long time. Then he whispered, "I saw him rise again as you two came out of the sacred lodge. He caught Tony as he was about to fall. He touched you, Rog, so that your feet scarcely brushed the ground. He danced on the water as the church folk sang, looking right pleased with himself for rising up again another year. The last I saw him, he was visiting some old 'friends' up on Shaman's Point."

He continued, "Well, Rog, you've fed your heart and soul and stomach. I think you should go home to your ma. Maybe you can search with a new heart for a forgiving home with your pa."

I rose from the table and paused uncertainly before Tony. I queried, "Now that I've got to be something more of a man, is it still all right for me to hug you, another man?"

He grabbed me in a bear hug. It certainly seemed more than all right. I guessed that this was what resurrection was really about—always finding new ways of being in touch.

I walked home in the morning sunlight. I paused at the straw cave. The whiskey bottle winked dully in the light. I picked it up. It was still a quarter full.

I knelt down and pled, "Forgive me, Mother Earth. I know I'm going to hurt you. I'm going to pour this whiskey into your embrace. Destroy the dark star people and take care of Tony."

I poured the dusky liquid into a rich, moist furrow. A tiny snake which I had not seen slithered quickly away. I crumbled soft loam over the offering site. I carried the bottle home with me.

I stepped into my father's shop. I would offer the object of evil and human devastation to—I wasn't quite sure to what or whom.

I laid the bottle on the anvil. I took a small hammer and carefully shattered it into as many pieces as possible. Then I took the sledge which I could barely lift and brought it down on the stack of glass. I beat the offending material to a fine sand. With each blow pictures of Tony's journey from the hell of the straw cave to resurrection morning registered on my mind screen.

With each blow I said my own prayer to the conjoint deities, Jesus and *Wakan Tanka*. I asked for freedom from the dark star people in Tony, in my daddy—and in me as well.

I brushed the ground sand-like glass into a little jar sitting on dad's workbench. I carried it into the house. Ma was peeling potatoes. She'd had Dad bring in a ham from the smokehouse the day before. An Easter feast was in the making. I kissed her wordlessly.

I stepped quietly past my father sitting with his head in his hands. He did not acknowledge my presence.

I paused for a moment, looked at him and then stepped to the icebox and chopped off a piece of frozen water gathered in winter from the holy lake. I wrapped it in a washcloth, stepped behind him and held it gently on his forehead.

My heart sang over and over:

May he live again, O Wakan Tanka.
Let the dark star people
Flee before your light.

He opened his eyes and grinned at me weakly. He said, "The cool of the cloth and the smell of that cookin' ham is enough to make a dead man walk."

He struggled to his feet. He seemed about to fall. I grabbed him in my arms and held him for a long moment.

He mumbled gruffly, "Thanks, kid. I guess it's a good thing yer' nearly as tall as yer old man. I must have had a touch of the flu. You kept me from fallin' flat on my face. I'd better git somethin' in my stomach to git me back some strength."

He stepped from my embrace to the nearby table. Tears were streaming down the cheeks of my watching mother.

Before dinner I walked into my bedroom and closed the door. I would leave the little jar on my bureau as a reminder to pray for Tony and my sick daddy. The world seemed suddenly alive with Holy Ones. Surely *Wakan Tanka* or the Thunderbird or the Risen Christ would be able to keep an eye on Tony.

Someone was listening. I never saw Tony Great Turtle drunk again.

INTERLUDE 4

Tony's body began a rhythmic movement from side to side. His hands flayed out, grasping the edge of the mattress. His face was a mask of agony. I was about to call for my Hermit Uncle John when, crying out in fear, Tony's eyes opened.

At the sound Uncle John came rushing into the room. He left quickly and returned with a cool washcloth to put on Tony's forehead. His fever must have skyrocketed again.

Tony said weakly, "I know I am living and dying in a dream world. But much of where we live and die is a dream world. Perhaps at last it is the better world."

I inquired, "Where were you, Tony?"

"I was on the ship *SS Nebraska*. March 31, 1887. The Wild West Show was sailing for England. There was great fear and much illness. I felt then as I do now, that death stands in the wings, waiting for my final performance."

John changed the washcloth. Tony seemed to rest easier.

The dim lamp enhaloed his face. He looked like one of the saints in the stained-glass window at St. Ignatius the Lesser.

Uncle John returned to his chair. I held the old man's hand and listened to the hallucinatory babble that flowed in and out of comprehension.

> *O Cody!*
> *Longhair Bill Cody!*
> *How many times must you kill my people?*
> *How many times must you kill my heart?*

Two hundred showpeople boarded the vessel...my heart was haunted by what the English would see...what they would think of us as a people...the ship was a place of terror...our tribal stories told of attacking monsters which would haunt us if we crossed the Great Water...that our flesh would gradually drop from our bones...we were terribly seasick, and the stench was overwhelming...we decided that nausea was the monster awaiting us...that would tear off our flesh.

Arriving in England, we went to the great gardens near Earl's Court...scenery had been painted on canvas so high it blotted out houses...a mountain pass had been constructed from which we could ride out and pillage...our tepees were clustered so that we could be stared at from many directions...Red Shirt was in charge of the Indians...the program said he had "intelligently accepted the situation since being conquered." *Hetchetu welo!*

We were Lakota in the company but were to be all the Plains Indians...sometimes I was Cheyenne, sometimes Arapahoe...we all knew we were playacting while the show was billed as "true in every detail."

The famous of England came to observe us...Gladstone, who had been prime minister, arrived with his entourage...the day was wet and very cold...he asked for a special showing of some of the riding...Cody called upon me to begin...clad only in breechclout I rode bareback before him, doing the daredevil...Gladstone wildly applauded and called me over to speak...I stood shivering before him as he spoke about riding...he paused mid-sentence, saying, "You're freezing, my child...I have an old greatcoat in the undertrunk of my carriage...I'll send someone for it"...everyone laughed when I slipped it on...my eagle feather rising royally above it...that coat now covers my dying.

Queen Victoria...her Diamond Jubilee was being celebrated...that's why we were in England...came out for entertainment to the Wild West Show...the first time in twenty-five years since the prince consort's death...Grandmother England gathered us 'round her...played with our babies unafraid...before she departed, she moved us all deeply by saying, "I am sixty seven years old. All over the world I have seen all kinds of people; but today I have seen the best–looking people I know. If you belonged to me, I would not let them take you around in a show like this."

Cody was a child who never grew up...he took London by

storm...everyone loved him...he lived out a fantasy that his world was true...that he was preparing his Indians for a better world than their own...that the West was as he portrayed it...but he didn't include scenes of life on the reservation to round out his picture. *Hetchetu welo!*

One night an old man approached me after the performance...he frightened me as he stared deep into my eyes..."Who are you?" he asked...I told him my name...that was not what he meant..."You are different from the others...I must know who you are...I watched you as you waited at the top of the canyon...you had time to reach upward, face to the heavens, palm stretching outward...what were you doing?"...my Mandan mother told of her people awaiting a blessing from the Spirit in All.

He smiled as he spoke, "My people, the Celts, stand with palm stretching outward awaiting a blessing...we feel the Spirit of holiness enlivening all things...there are spirits in rivers, in rocks and in mountains...we have places of holiness where the spirits meet and we meet the spirits."

My heart grew sad at the memory...the memory of our sacred hills sold to the white man...I told him the story...he understood...he was from a tribe called the Welsh...their sacred places were conquered as well.

I felt a brotherness with the strange man before me...he asked me again who I was...I told him I was part Lakota and part Mandan...his face lighted with joy..."There is an old tale which few believe...that Welsh Prince Madog with twelve boats of followers sailed to the New World...mixed with the peoples...became the strange tribe called Mandan who share ways of building and worship with those in Wales."

I told him that the Mandans had been nearly all killed by smallpox...his face grew sad, yet he smiled, "If the legend is true, they may have been my people, and you are my brother." I laughed and gave him my hand.

He asked if I was Christian...I assured him I was not...then I asked if he was...he replied, "Yes and no. We name the living spirit reborn every year the Christ-presence. We try to live out his love and his story in our own way so that we can keep seeing the Spirit in all."

I told him of Wakan Tanka and of all of our Holy Ones...we decided that his Christ and our Holy Ones would enjoy being at one table...they would laugh and eat and dance together.

He took my hand, saying, "Even if Madog did not sail, you are still my brother"...he disappeared in the darkness...to meet a brother who saw me as a whole person...not a mere savage from the American West...my heart sang within me...I walked to a garden...stood beneath a great oak and sang to Wakan Tanka:

Mitakuye oyasin: We are all related!
Mitakuye oyasin: We are all related!

If the wasichu could only understand...if Bill Cody could have understood...we do not have to become like them to be related.

O Cody!
Longhair Bill Cody!
Generations have passed
And I must forgive you.

Tony's hand moved to the worn greatcoat which covered him. He stroked it lovingly as fatigue overcame him. He moved from a wordless chant to the world of sleep.

I changed the washcloth on his forehead and dozed at his side.

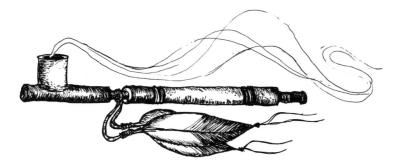

A PARTY TO SAVE ME

His imperious finger pointed to the sidelines of the football field. Bandmaster Sherm Savola nailed me with his fiery dark eyes which were usually limpid pools of romantic darkness, especially in the presence of certain female teachers. Now their Vesuvian fire melted away any hope I had of marching in the Labor Day football game between the Pheasant Valley Foxes and the Maple Grove Redskins which traditionally opened the sports season.

As I turned slowly to obey his command, I saw Cleola Adkins smirking from her position of power gained from my downfall. The sun glinted from her brand-new gold-toned instrument. She was now head of the clarinet section—temporarily, I hoped.

Savola's harsh words caused snickers throughout the marching ensemble: "I don't know what's gotten into you, Rog. You're missing half the notes and you don't seem to know your right foot from your left. Forget about Friday's game. Don't bother to report for practice until next Monday."

I was devastated. It was only Tuesday. Next to my Hermit Uncle John and Tony Great Turtle's occasional appearances, music was my chief source of escape and healing.

The band's derisive snickers flicked switches in my psyche. All the schoolyard taunts ever tossed at me shaped themselves into an epic chorus in my head:

> Hey! Bucktooth, stammerin' Rog,
> Playin' dodge ball, you can't dodge,

In keep-away you're always "it,"
Bucktooth Rog is havin' a fit.

I imagined girls in the elementary school playground across the street skipping rope to those immortal rhythms. I slunk under the bleachers, put my instrument in its case, picked up my books and headed into Pheasant Valley. I wouldn't wait for the team bus that took country players home late. I'd walk across the fields, braving my father's anger when I arrived too late to assist with the chores.

My father's wrath had really been the cause of this whole sorry affair. His darknesses were coming with increasing frequency. Their duration was shorter. As a consequence, however, Mom and I were subjected more often than usual to the brutality that accompanied his descents into terrible silent depression.

The previous Sunday afternoon Dad and I had been repairing a hoghouse behind the barn. We waded through the odorous muck to the side of the shed where a sow had rooted off a board. Dad was on a rapid descent and his blistering temper boiled just below the surface.

I was determined to do everything possible to please him. I was carrying the board. He had a hammer in one hand and a few nails in the other.

He commanded, "You hold the board in place real straight so's there won't be any crack. I don't want no cold air blowin' through and givin' the newborns pneumonia. We gotta' git the lead out. It's cloudin' up and I want to git this done 'afore the storm hits."

I squatted down, focussing on my task. I forced the board's lip into the groove of the one above. I pushed too hard. My feet slipped out from under me. I found myself face-down in the manure-saturated mud, a corncob scraping my cheek, my fingers splayed out on the fallen board.

I waited for the torrent of profanity to push me further down into the accumulated abusive muck within my soul. There was terrible silence. It was completed by two nerve-shattering bursts of pain, one in each hand.

He had smashed my fingers by a couple of short, hard strikes with the flat side of the steel hammerhead. The action released his torrent of destructive words as he strode across the yard, removing himself from my worthless presence as fast as possible.

Dad wasn't watching where he was going. Just as I raised myself from the mud, he caught his foot on the low edge of a feeding trough. He plummeted to the rain-soaked earth which had been stirred into a swamp by the snouts of rooting pigs.

With a sucking sound, he separated himself from the roiled earth. He stood up. He hissed out his most constant basic phrases embroidered with unbelievable profanity, "As usual, this is all your fault, you worthless little bastard."

He stood there, mud-covered, looking every inch a swamp monster from one of the worn comic books a cousin occasionally passed my way. He was silhouetted against the barn. My eyes went to the point of the gable. Maybe Batman, or Captain Marvel, or Superman, or *Wakan Tanka* in the form of Thunderbird or even the angel Gabriel would suddenly materialize and zap my raging daddy.

No savior appeared against the glowering clouds. Instead, I watched in frozen terror as Dad s-l-o-w-l-y pulled back his hammer-bearing right hand. I knew I was about to be a target. I panicked. Last fall at the county fair he'd joined in the hammer-throwing contest. He'd won a kewpie doll. At least this time he wasn't about to throw a sledgehammer.

I quickly balled myself up to protect the most vulnerable parts of my body. The missile smashed head first into my left knee. My stomach heaved. My lunch joined the rest of the debris in that rank yard.

Pain flowed through my body from knee to fingers like motifs in a discordant symphony. My father turned and lumbered slowly off, his feet partially imprisoned in the black ooze.

I slipped into semi-consciousness. Playing in the haze of my mind was a vision of Dad being slowly sucked into the hogyard morass and disappearing forever into the Hades of my beloved

Greek mythology.

I was snapped back to reality by a gentle nuzzling at my mud-buried right cheek. An old brood sow was rooting my face out of the muck as if it were a strayed piglet. Her rough snout was the softest touch I'd known in a long time.

I struggled slowly to my feet. I swayed as the dizzying pain in my knee struck with renewed ferocity. I reached out to steady myself against the hoghouse wall. I discovered that I couldn't flatten out my hand. The fingers were badly swollen.

I slogged across the farmyard to the huge watering tank near the windmill. The water would be cold. I cleaned the muck from my fingers on the lush grass growing around the tank. I plunged my hands in the cool water. The relief was ecstatic. I wished I could simply climb into the tank. However, it would not be fair to the innocent cows and horses for me to foul their water.

I stepped up onto the low platform surrounding the pump beneath the windmill tower. A gale was blowing. It looked as if the impending storm was going to go around us.

From a small bucket I poured some water down the pump to prime it. Its bail bit painfully into my battered hand. I released the lever which controlled the head of the windmill. Its blades spun. Water began to flow from the pump spout. I held my hands beneath the cold gush. The pain lessened.

I filled the bucket and stepped off the platform so the filth from my body would not run down into the clear well. I poured the icy liquid over my head. Six buckets later I felt clean again.

I couldn't let the windmill pump forever or the well would run momentarily dry. I pulled the lever down. It hummed into silence.

The pain continued to course through my body along the connective nerves. I stepped to the stock tank, removed my clothes and shoes, and lowered myself into the cooling waters. The curious cattle approached and ringed the tank. They mooed softly at the strange intruder. I laid my head on my arms on the side of the tank with my shattered hands beneath the water. For the first time that day I wept.

The next morning I got up early to milk my cows before school. Dad was sleeping fitfully in the old oak rocking chair. Mom had not bothered to get him to bed.

I limped to the barn. My hands were painfully stiff. Some of my fingertips were still swollen.

It was agony to squeeze down the cows' teats to release the milk. My knee protested bending as I crouched on the three-legged milking stool. I knew I had to get myself limbered up. The band was working on some new marching routines. I was to do a special clarinet obbligato on "Under the Double Eagle." We were also being "scouted" by a judge from the University of Minnesota to see whether we were good enough to march in a massed band in the halftime show of their homecoming game.

I got to school. We had band first period. I heard Cleola Adkins practicing *my* solo. She was terrible!

Yet Cleola was a real threat. We were always battling for the first chair position. It was grudgingly admitted that, strange as I was, I was the best clarinetist ever produced by Pheasant Valley High.

The threat came not because of her music but because of her mother. Midge Adkins taught girls physical education. She was a shapely brunette with the longest eyelashes in the county.

She'd gone away and gotten an education. When she came back and married Tock Adkins who worked for the county highway department, there was a general feeling that she'd "married beneath her."

Then, when the members of the Ladies Aid at the Baptist Church of Peter-the-Rock counted on their fingers from the wedding day to Cleola's birth, they never made it to nine months. However, Midge's mother assured anyone who would listen that the baby had been "a bit premature." The other women exchanged arched eyebrows behind her back.

Eight years later Tock Adkins "mysteriously" disappeared and was never heard from again. The mystery was somewhat mitigated when Chitty Bigelow who tended bar at the Dew Drop

Inn also "mysteriously" disappeared. Nothing was ever proved. Midge kept her own tight-lipped counsel.

When Midge graced the gym or the playing field in her chastely revealing uniforms, Sherm Savola had eyes only for her, to the disgruntlement of the other unmarried female teachers. The high school boys looked forward to those occasional times when the two classes met together for "folk dancing" under her instruction. They gave her their strictest attention.

Midge never returned Sherm's not-so-subtle overtures until Cleola began to advance through the chairs in the clarinet section. There was a general feeling in the community that Midge pushed Cleola to be the best in all her classes, to be president of Job's Daughters and Future Homemakers of America and, hopefully, to be first-chair clarinetist.

Sherm was heard to comment that he'd do just about anything to "get close" to Midge. Then Cleola began to move up the music ranks with amazing rapidity. It was rumored that Sherm and Midge had been seen dining at the Twilight Supper Club in nearby Pleasant Plain. A sub-rumor had it that they'd each had a glass of white wine at their table. A single rose in a vase decorated her place setting.

The rumors arose because Herb and Helena Henkel were celebrating their thirty-third wedding anniversary three tables over. Helena later commented slyly to Letitia Fogarty, "It was downright amazing just how often Mr. Savola had to reach over and tenderly brush crumbs of the Club's prize Russian Pumpernickel from Midge's cheeks or lips. One would think she was old enough to use her own napkin."

Letitia acknowledged that one would so think. Soon the town was abuzz with speculation.

Walking into the band room, I tried desperately to disguise my limp. Mr. Savola had a pained expression on his face as he listened from a distance to Cleola butchering "The Double Eagle." She abruptly stopped her invasion of my solo and shot an innocent blank-faced look in my direction.

I assembled my instrument. Some of my fingers were still

too swollen to fit tightly over the air holes. I produced a series of shrill bleeps. Mr. Savola and the arriving students looked at me strangely.

I stopped trying and headed for the boys' bathroom. I ran cold water over my hands and prayed for instantaneous healing to my entire pantheon of deities: Greek, Roman, Judeo-Christian and Lakota. Nothing worked.

Mr. Savola took us immediately to the field. We lined up. He explained the first maneuver. Every left turn was sheer agony. I could almost walk straight without a limp, but I broke step on the turns.

I didn't dare tell him what the problem was. My mother had sworn me to silence about my daddy's violence.

It was even worse when he asked me to inspire the band with my Sousa march solo. Again, the bleeps. The entire ensemble broke out in laughter.

When he inquired about what was wrong, I told him I'd taken a little fall but would be fine tomorrow. He said severely, "Well, I hope so. You're holding the whole band back."

My fear of failure made the following day even worse. He ordered me off the field, and Cleola's star rose still higher in the Pheasant Valley sky. I glanced back. The band was taking a five-minute break. Sherm was looking over to the next playing field where the girls track team was practicing under Midge's enthusiastic coaching. A little smile played about his lips. Just then Cleola passed him. He gave her a reassuring nod.

I dawdled through the main street of town. I paused at the great open lot by the gas station. In preparation for the community Labor Day celebration, the carnival was in the process of setting up just west of the gas station's sign of the flying red horse. The same show came every year: Blind Ben See's Carnival of Wonders. If Blind Ben did not get enough bookings, he sometimes played a few days in early summer as well.

The first tent to be raised was the fun house. Blind Ben, dressed all in black like a preacher man, sat in a gilded chair on the fun house platform in front of the Mirror of Truth which blew you up and shriveled you down as you walked by. There was one tiny spot where you looked normal if you hit it right.

Though Ben couldn't see, he supervised his enterprise from this place of honor and took tickets when the show was operating. Everybody said he had an interior "third eye" that allowed him to know what was going on in an uncanny fashion.

I stood at the foot of the platform and watched him closely. His head moved back and forth as if he could see the tents rising and the rides being assembled.

I was startled by him addressing me: "Hey, young man. The show's not open yet. Why don't you come on up and have a free look in the mirror. It probably wouldn't hurt a gimpy-legged boy at all."

I froze. How did he know that I was limping? Then I remembered that folks said because of his blindness his hearing had developed so he could catch any sound "a mile away." I had no explanation, however, for how he knew I was a young man.

I stumbled up onto the platform. As I brushed past him, he reached out and took my arm and maneuvered me into the spot where you saw yourself as you are. He commented, "It feels the way you're shakin' you don't need to be torn apart any more."

What I saw in the mirror was a pretty sorry sight: a lanky kid in bib overalls with a faded blue chambray shirt and heavy front-laced blutcher shoes. My face was pale. My eyes had dark circles under them.

Suddenly, I was not alone in the mirror. A figure came into focus behind me. His worn denim clothing, his leather hat with the eagle feather and his long braids were unmistakable. It was Tony Great Turtle.

I spun around and rushed into his arms sobbing with relief. Blind Ben commented wryly, "It sounds as if the youngster has run into an old acquaintance."

When I got hold of myself, I queried, "T-T-Tony, what are you d-doin' here in the c-c-carnival?"

Ben answered for him: "Tony and I go back to days together in Bill Cody's Wild West Show. That was before I got religion and lost it again—at least the church kind. I bought this show twenty years ago. It gives me a living and a place for Tony to hide out when he needs one."

I didn't even ask what he meant by that. I said, "T-Tony, we've got to t-talk. I h-h-hurt so b-bad outside and i-inside I don't think I c-c-can m-make it."

He responded, "Let's just sit down on the edge of the platform. It won't hurt none if Ben hears what you got to say."

I told them the entire story of my battering at home and at school.

There was a long silence. Tony said softly, "Ben, we need to take this boy on a little journey. Why don't you leave the setup for a couple of hours. Get one of the roustabouts to drive us a few miles out in the country. Besides, Ben, there's somebody I've always wanted you to meet."

I replied with delight, "Y-You m-m-mean my Hermit Uncle J-J-John!"

Tony smiled, "You're right. I think an old bareback rider turned preacher turned carney, a fugitive shaman and a hermit driven to holiness by the terror of war—well, I think the three of us should be able to put this big overgrown Humpty-Dumpty together again."

Ben called to a short, swarthy dark-haired man: "Hey, Dingo. I need you to drive us someplace for a couple of hours. Take us out, come on back and finish assembling the ferris wheel and then pick us up again before dark."

Tony disappeared for a few moments. When he returned, he had his familiar worn leather bag with him.

We were dropped off at the head of the lane leading to the lakeshore. The silent Dingo drove off.

As we walked down the ruts, Ben kept his fingers lightly on Tony's arm. It was obvious they had traveled many miles together.

John's little dog Tiny came bursting out of the bushes as we neared the shack. She set up a commotion that brought John to the bottom of the path.

John moved toward Tony, stammering in excitement, "I-I-I-I was b-beginning to th-th-think you were never c-coming back. It's b-b-been such a l-long time!"

The old men embraced. Tony turned, took Ben's hand and placed it in John's. He said, "I want you to meet Rog's uncle, John Robbennolt."

Ben commented, "You're very tall. I feel it in your hand." I felt bad for my Uncle John. He'd once been six-foot-four. But the terror of war and long years alone had shrunk him down to about five-eleven.

Tony laughed. "Every once in awhile I wonder if you really are blind and then you make a comment that assures me you are. John is real tall all right: inside, where it counts."

I was leaning against a tree trying to get my leg in a position that was comfortable. John looked at me closely and asked, "Did that brother of mine hurt you again?"

"Y-Yes. I've b-b-been hurt lots of ways the last coupla' days."

Tony intervened: "That's why we're here. I think we have a little healing to do. We can't let this young man fall back into self-pity. He'll never grow beyond hate if we let him do that. I have an idea or two."

He turned to me and said, "Go to the sweat lodge site. Take the bucket and the sage branch from there to the lake. Fill it and bring it to Shaman's Point. John, bring a loaf of your fine bread up with you. Ben and I will meet you both at the tip of the Point."

I protested, "There's n-no way I can w-w-walk all the way up to Shaman's Point carrying anything h-heavy."

Tony gave me a long look. He said, "We're searching for a path through and beyond your pain. There's always a way. Go!"

I went. Walking over the rough ground, my leg throbbed. As I retrieved the bucket and filled it from the sacred lake, the bail cut into my swollen fingers. The top of the sage branch floating in the bucket kept irritating the underside of my arm. Stumbling up the narrow path, I changed the pail from hand to hand. I nearly fell as my knee gave way. Sobs rose in my throat. What kept me going was the thought that something special awaited me at the tip of the Shaman's Point. Tony and John had never failed me. I also felt a strange confidence in the old blind man.

There at the top of the rock the red fire burned. The smell of sage and sweet grass called forth a host of memories of times when it had been burned in my presence. The pain lessened.

The three men were facing west over the lake. Tony was chanting in Lakota. As I approached, they turned toward me, their arms extended in welcome. I walked hesitantly up to them. Tony received the water and placed it on a bench-like outcropping near the edge of the point next to a magnificent loaf of John's bread. Between them stood the abalone shell with a smudge of sage and sweet grass burning in it.

My Hermit Uncle John guided Blind Ben See's left hand to my right shoulder. He placed his right hand on my left shoulder. Tony stood before me. He said, "Hate keeps welling up inside you. I think you've forgotten about breathing in the stars. Maybe we can plant some seeds within you that will take better root. We're about to make you a *hunka*, a beloved one. This is a most sacred ceremony. If you can only remember it, you need never hate your daddy, or Mr. Savola, or Cleola or anyone else again. Hate boils up only when you can't stand yourself."

I thought for a moment and then said, "I'm willing to try anything, Tony. Make me into somebody who can see through pain and beyond hate. I get real tired hating."

He picked up the abalone shell. Removing the eagle feather from his hat, he fanned the herbs into a rich smudge. He offered it in the four directions and to the heavens and the earth. He smudged the entire length of my body from head to foot. I held out my arms and he smudged them. Then he smudged himself, John and Ben.

He turned to the bucket of sacred water. He cupped his hands and filled them. He let it dribble slowly over my head. Some of it soaked my shirt. The lake breezes cooled me. I shivered. The pain was not as intense.

He massaged the water into my hair and sang:

> *Grandmother Earth, hear me!*
> *Upon you we are remaking this boy*
> *On the edge of manhood,*
> *Just as you have remade us*
> *By bringing to us our sacred pipe.*
> *The two-leggeds, the four-leggeds, the wingeds,*
> *And all that move upon you are your children.*
> *With all beings and with all things he and we*
> *shall be as relatives;*
> *Just as we are related to you, O Mother,*
> *So shall we make peace with all people*
> *and shall be related to them.*
> *May we walk with love and mercy upon that path.*

A rabbit quivered under a hazelnut bush at the edge of the path. Ravens hung motionless in the air above us like a congregation observing a sacrament.

Tony took the sage branch and sprinkled me with water. He handed it to Uncle John and Ben in turn. As they shook water lightly upon me, Tony intoned:

> *Wakan Tanka, cleanse him into joy.*
> *Wakan Tanka, cleanse him into joy.*
> *Wakan Tanka, cleanse him into joy.*

I felt incredibly light. In spite of the cool water the brilliant rays of the sun seemed to penetrate to the very heart of my deep-seated despair about everything in my life.

Tony reached into his bag and pulled out two little pots of paint. He first daubed vermilion on my face and smoothed it out. I felt him circle the red with a thin line of blue. He overlaid a blue line on my forehead, on both cheekbones and on my chin.

He motioned for me to be seated on the rock bench. Again, Tony filled his cupped hands with water. He held them to my lips. I bent forward to drink. He quickly pulled back his hands. He chanted:

> *As a hunka, one beloved,*
> *You can no longer think only of yourself;*

> When you would hastily quench your own thirst,
>   You shall stop and look about you
> for those who are faint and weary.
>   Of those you must be mindful.
> Then you may drink.

Tony held the water to my lips. I drank.

He broke off a piece of bread, passed it through the smudge and broke it in two. He threw one piece into the sacred red fire and placed the other piece on my tongue. The chant resumed:

> Whenever you eat,
>   Remember that someone may be hungering
>   for a morsel of your food.
>   Remember what you have become here.
> When you eat,
>   Stop the food midway to your lips
>   and remember,
> You shall not eat your food alone.
>   You shall eat half a morsel.
>   With the other you shall show mercy.
>   May *Wakan Tanka* walk with you
> So you may be unafraid.

I chewed the bread and swallowed it. Without any prompting from Tony, I broke off pieces from the loaf, honored the fire and placed some bread on each of the men's tongues. I gave them cupped handfuls of water. Tony smiled.

The ravens burst into discordant song and settled joyfully in the great black walnut tree. The rabbit scampered down the path.

Blind Ben See and my Hermit Uncle John hugged me close.

Tony reached into his bag again and pulled out the sacred deerskin. He wrapped it loosely around me. His song rose in high ululations—his tongue quivering as the shrill sounds emerged.

As he sang, he picked up the abalone shell which was now cold. John and Ben each took one of my hands and dipped it in the water. Then they touched my injured fingers one at a time to the ashes from the sacred herbs.

My Hermit Uncle John knelt and lifted the left leg of my overalls. He gently stroked ashes on my damaged knee.

They each again sprinkled me with the branch of sage. The song stopped. Tony removed the deerskin from my shoulders. I stared at my fingertips. There was not a trace of swelling. I tentatively placed my full weight on my left leg. There was no pain.

I floated for a moment in an unbelieving trance. I visioned myself standing in the middle of the high school football field, the band around me in a diamond formation. I swung into my clarinet solo, embellishing the printed cascade of notes with runs and trills never dreamed of by John Philip Sousa. My fingers flew over the keys with uncanny alacrity. My legs moved in a marching strut that gave lie to my essential lack of coordination. I finished the solo and marched brightly to the tip of the diamond for a well-deserved bow. Pandemonium erupted in the bleachers as my performance was acknowledged. Even the fans from rival Maple Grove shouted their *bravos*.

I was brought back to the present by Uncle John's little dog, Tiny, playing a ferocious game with my pant leg as I marched in place. Tony, Ben and John stood grinning broadly. They were three wise fools proud of their joint participation in Tony's foolish wisdom.

In the distance a horn honked. We were awaited at the end of the lane. I asked Tony, "May I use the rest of the water in the bucket to wash the paint from my face?"

He said in a voice of mystery, "Not until you've seen your father."

"He'll kill me for sure!" I exploded.

He only repeated more firmly, "Not until you've seen your father."

We helped him repack his bag. The horn sounded more insistently.

We bid John farewell.

Our progress was quicker this time. I ran ahead of the two old men.

When we climbed into the car, Dingo stared at me for a moment. His eyes widened. He said not a word but drove stolidly along the gravel road in the first rays of sunset.

I was dropped off at our farm. I retrieved my clarinet from the back seat of the car and headed down our driveway. In the distance I saw my dad feeding the pigs. I hesitated. I squared my shoulders and walked on. After all, I was a *hunka*, a beloved one who shared and was unafraid.

My dog, Skippy, came out to greet me. He took one look at my face and went howling through the poplar trees in the windbreak.

I paused at the house. Maybe I could really scare my ma. I slipped in only to find a note: "I've gone to give a hand with Bartie Maclett's seventh baby. There's chicken fried and fresh biscuits. Warm up some peas and potatoes for you and your dad."

I had to face my father. As I went out the back door, I got the first good look at myself in the cracked mirror that hung above the chipped white enamel wash basin. I couldn't believe my eyes. A figure from the dawn of time stared back. I thought, "So that's a *hunka*. Somebody who's supposed to be wonderful but weird. But maybe you've got to be a little weird as the world sees you before you can follow all of Tony's good instructions."

I headed for the barnyard.

Dad was standing by the watering tank, watching it fill as the windmill turned and the pump jack drew up the water.

I stepped behind him and said quietly, "Sorry I'm late, Dad."

He swung around angrily, caught sight of my face and gasped out, "What the Sam Hill?..."

An enormous guffaw burst from the center of his belly. Another followed. He laughed so hard that tears ran down his face. He pointed at me, slapped his thigh and laughed some more.

The guzzling cattle backed away from the tank in dumb amazement at this unaccustomed sound echoing through the farmyard.

Dad walked up to me, grabbed me by the hair, and bent my head back, not in anger but in jest. "If you ain't somethin'. I ain't laughed that hard in years. I feel great. I won't even ask you where you got that bogeyman face. Just come on up to the house, and I'll help you get it off. I may need to use Bon Ami cleanser."

He loosed my hair, put an arm around my shoulders and walked me up to the house. Leaving me outside, he took the washbasin and filled it with warm water from the reservoir on the cookstove.

He came out with a new bar of homemade soap to which my mother had added a touch of mint, a wash cloth and a soft towel. Setting the pan on its crate, Dad soaped up the cloth. I expected to be attacked and the skin scrubbed off my face. To my amazement his post-laughter touch was as gentle as Tony's, as caring as my Hermit Uncle John's. For the first time I sensed Dad and John were brothers.

He lighted the lantern to hold back the gathering dark. He gave my face about three more washings and decided to call it quits, commenting, "Folks may be able to see a few shadows in the sunlight. That'll just confuse 'em."

We went inside. He'd finished the milking without me. While he ran the separator, I fried potatoes and heated the peas. When we were ready, I removed the chicken and the baking-powder biscuits from the still-warm oven.

Dad brought in a pitcher of fresh milk. We usually ate our supper by the dim light of the smoky wall-mounted lamp over the stove. While I finished dishing up the food, he stepped into the living room and brought out the good Aladdin lamp which was only lighted for company, commenting as he came, "Thought it might be a good idea to really see what we're eating for once."

I felt like a guest, a beloved person. While he loaded his plate with potatoes, peas and biscuits, I dove into the platter of chicken and removed both drumsticks. I had one almost to my mouth when I remembered. I quickly said, "Sorry, Dad. I almost forgot: you like drumsticks too."

I reached across the table and put one on his plate. He grinned his thanks.

It was truly a sacramental meal.

The following morning I got up extra early, finished my milking, caught a ride into town with Crist Creeder who worked at the Farmers' Co-op Creamery and arrived at school before anyone else. Axel Mattson, the aging janitor, let me in after I assured him that I had an hour's special practicing to do.

I stepped into the band room. When I flipped on the light, the first thing I noticed was Cleola's leather music folder on the first-chair clarinet stand. One of her long, wide red-velvet hair ribbons was draped over the stand as if to add a royal touch to her recently conquered musical kingdom.

My battered cardboard folder had been summarily shoved into second place. I sat down and opened it. I pulled out the music for the solo. I realized that I didn't need it. I flowed the music in a wild ripple of sound rivaling my soundless performance from the day before.

I played it over and over, varying the patterns and dynamic colorations. The sound sang through the entire school. My spirit soared. I was unaware that arriving teachers and early students were gathering in the back of the room.

I finally ran out of breath. The room erupted in applause. I was aware of someone at my side. It was Cleola. She was weaving the red ribbon into her long blond braid. Wordlessly, she exchanged our folders. She had tears in her eyes.

I remembered that I was *hunka*. I turned to her and said softly, "I think I could probably teach you the fingering before tomorrow night's game."

She eyed me quizzically and said, "I couldn't play like that in a hundred years. You were playing as if you were bewitched!"

Now that she mentioned it, did I not feel a "friend" or two from Shaman's Point caressing my hands as I played?

I turned to see Sherm Savola sadly watching the disappearing figure of Midge Adkins. There was a definitive note of angry belligerence in the sound of her high heels striking the tile floor of the long, echoing hall.

INTERLUDE 5

The wind raged outside the cabin. Within, a strange calm presided over the approaching death of Tony Great Turtle. The great clock struck nine. I had slipped out and gotten *Grimm's Fairy Tales*. I strained to read by the low light of the wall-mounted kerosene lamp.

I glanced up. Tony's eyes were watching me closely. He said, "You must read everything. You must learn everything there is to know about people. Then you will live as a *hunka*, a true hope-bringer. Now, be a good *hunka*. Dip your finger in the water and moisten my lips. I do not want to raise my head."

I moistened his lips. The fever had baked them to a sandpaper-like quality.

His eyes closed. Again, mumbled words swirled from his lips. I think I heard most of them. He seemed to be reminiscing about Sitting Bull after the set litany which always began his death's-door ramblings.

O Cody!
Longhair Bill Cody!
How many times must you kill my people?
How many times must you kill my heart?

You could have saved him...Sitting Bull...he loved you...named you first, Pehaska, Longhair...traveled with the show in 1885...the West's most dangerous Indian leader...so the government reasoned...he was a fine, stubborn man who resisted reservations...a shaman in his own way...when the Ghost Dancers moved across the country, the fear was that Sitting Bull would lead the destruction of the wasichu.

You could have saved him...you knew there was a plan somewhere for his condemnation...in Washington the Great White Father feared the Ghost Dancers...had lists sent of the fomenters of the revolution...Sitting Bull was on the list...you were sent for by General Nelson Miles...to bring in the chief personally...you knew you could do it by presents and persuasion...then McLaughlin, the Standing Rock agent, doubting your skills called President Harrison...he canceled your orders returning you to Chicago.

You could have saved him if you'd left your followers and come quickly alone...you could have saved him if you'd slipped away to see him on the reservation...you were busy with your party...you never heard the gunshot...fired by his own kind...bullets came from Bull Head and Red Tomahawk...his lifeless body lay in his cabin yard, surrounded by police of his own kind...the end to a leader...a leader of his people.

His death brought defeat to the spirit of the Ghost Dance...leading to the Massacre at Wounded Knee...you could have saved them, Longhair Bill Cody...you could have saved Sitting Bull.

And when they jailed a hundred dancers for refusing the reservation, you had them released to travel with your show...they did not know how they would be portrayed...you finally added the Battle of Little Big Horn...At last the Indians won...this gave audiences a chance to boo the Indians for their "savagery" to Custer. Hetchetu welo!

O Cody!
Longhair Bill Cody!
Generations have passed
And I must forgive you.

He whispered himself into a deep sleep. I wished there was something I could do to allow him to forgive Bill Cody. Cody thought he was doing a fine thing killing buffalo, putting Indians on reservations and starting a Wild West show. I wonder what would happen, dear Tony, if you ever fully forgave him.

I went back to my book to read tales of far away and long ago. Unlike Cody, I could return from fantasy. He had lived it.

Tony's body gave a great jerk. I went to him and held him. My shoulders would ache, but I would not feel the pain. It was my gift of love to a fading Tony.

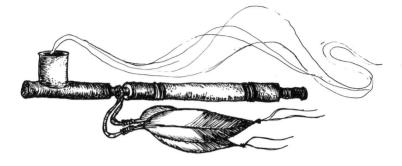

TO DANCE AS A MAN

It was late in the Moon when Calves Grow Hair (September). The temperature unexpectedly skyrocketed into the low nineties.

The summer drought was severe, lowering the water in the holy lake. Tony Great Turtle and I had to walk much further out into the water for our pre-sweat-lodge ceremonial cleansing.

The moon was full. It transformed the world into a place of dancing light and shadows. We slipped our heads beneath the water for a moment. We came up ready for the next step of transformation into new beings within the sweat lodge itself.

I kept asking Tony if we hadn't already become what we were going to become. He chided me for my impatience, saying, "It never happens all at once, and never fully happens until the scenery changes in our journey at that time called death."

He paused for a moment and then added quietly, "I feel that change is beginning to happen within me. My visions are richer. The Old Ones call me. The voices on Shaman's Point keep hungering for me to join them."

As we waded to shore, Tony sang a chant which he had learned from Crazy Horse:

> *My friend,*
> > *They will return again.*
> *All over the earth,*
> > *They are returning again.*
> *Ancient teachings of the Earth,*

Ancient songs of the Earth,
They are returning again.

I knew they were returning to me through Tony. I felt proud and scared. Tony turned to me and said simply, "Tonight, I hope you will learn something of the secret of dancing like a man."

My Hermit Uncle John was tending the sacred rock fire. He would never join us in the sweat lodge. He would look embarrassed and stammer out, "I-I'd just r-r-rather be a servant on the ou-ou-ou-outside."

Tony would always light the sacred herbs in the abalone shell before entering the lodge and smudge the three of us together. He assured Uncle John that he was the most holy man of all. The old hermit grinned with pleasure.

On this night we paused for a moment on the launching rock, drinking in the beauty of the world. Tony turned to me and said in hushed tones, "All is *wakan.*"

As the light fully illumined him, the scars on each of his breasts flamed in a way I had never seen before. I gasped.

He smiled. "That is a sure sign that death is moving closer. It is said that on such an occasion, the holy marks upon one's body fill with the Spirit and dance when touched with sacred light."

We moved to the lodge which we had placed in readiness earlier in the afternoon. I was starved. Tony insisted that we had to fast to be fully prepared for any visions with which *Wakan Tanka* might gift us. I would have preferred visions on a full stomach. However, a kid does not argue with a shaman.

Uncle John stood waiting by the glowing rocks. He held the antlers to transport the stones. The bucket of holy water from the lake was at his feet. As we neared the fire, preparing to walk the ten steps on the sacred path from fire pit to lodge, I was overcome by another smell which nearly blotted out the odors of twisted sweetgrass and the sage gathered in the sacred manner. I couldn't identify the intruding smell but it sharpened my hunger.

I saw Tony direct a quizzical glance at my Hermit Uncle John who dropped his eyes in what approached mock shame. I saw a suggestion of a smile play on Tony's lips as he stepped through the east-facing entrance to the lodge. I followed.

In the ritual steps of the *inipi*, we rubbed ourselves with water. The hot rocks had been doused a third time. As Tony turned, the glow from the rocks caught fire on his scars.

He began to talk. His voice wandered through the past, through bits of visions and disconnected chants. Lakota and English intermingled. Finally, he focused on words I had heard many times. He said they too had come from Crazy Horse:

> My friend,
>> They are coming back.
> In a sacred way,
>> All over the universe,
> Behold, they are coming back.
> The whole universe
>> Moving in a sacred way.
> Behold, over there,
>> From the spirit world,
> They are coming back.
>> Over the whole universe,
> Behold, they are coming back.

"My great-grandmother, training me in the deepest of sacred ways, said I could bring them back more quickly if I set myself always on the path of holiness. I have sometimes stepped off that path. When I went with Longhair Bill Cody's Wild West Show, I was far from the path.

"But since I once had done the deepest, most sacred thing, the Sun Dance, I could hope to return to the path.

"When I was a child, the Old Ones told of how one man saved our people. It was at least two thousand years ago. Game disappeared from the earth. The people were dying.

"The man received a special vision from *Wakan Tanka*. He was to drag a gigantic buffalo skull fastened by a thong to a peg driven through the flesh of his back. With the help of friends he prepared himself.

"Then he began to walk. He never stopped to eat or drink. For four days he kept walking, never pausing for mountains, storm or streams.

"On the fourth day he broke loose. Animals appeared on the plains. The people were saved."

I looked at Tony for a long moment: "That's kinda' similar to what Jesus did at about the same time in history—in terms of bein' pierced and breakin' loose and savin' folk."

Tony was silent. He turned to me, his old face wrinkled into a wry grin: "I never thought of that before. It makes me even more convinced that Jesus visits different people in different ways."

He gripped my shoulder in tender camaraderie and then continued, "When I come here to the site of my ancient people, I return to the path in a special way. I am instructed by our 'friends' on the tip of Shaman's Point."

I inquired, "Tony, are you ever going to teach me to do a Sun Dance? I need all the help I can get to stick to some sort of sacred path."

I heard his breath catch in the darkness lighted only with the faint glow of the rocks. Sweat was pouring from us. I was afraid he might faint. Tony responded, "I think you've done a Sun Dance without knowing it."

There was a long silence. Something in me wanted to press him to explain. For once in my life I controlled my tongue. I was about to be walked to the center of Mystery.

Tony began chanting again. A story rose from his rhythmic outcries: "I swung there for hours...swung on the Tree that Talks the Wind, the cottonwood...1877...I was twenty years old when I swung there.

"I sought true holiness...the holiness of the shaman...I could not simply dance on Earth, our Mother, till the shards pulled from my flesh...I had to swing between Grandfather Sky and Mother Earth.

The *wakan* which flowed from both sustained me as I swung...swung for hours from the sacred tree set by the tribe in the encampment's center...blowing, when I had breath, on my sacred whistle made from the eagle's wing, decorated with quills of porcupine and scales of carp...so that I might be sustained by the winged ones and the walking ones and the water ones.

"Swinging between earth and heaven, the *wakan* of all creation filled me...gave me strength to bear the blood loss from the cherry wood stakes driven through my breasts by Spirit Stone, the holy man in charge of dancer preparation...I did not wince when my flesh was gathered, knife inserted, stakes slipped through...my wounds purified by sage and sweetgrass.

"I walked beneath the sacred tree, the singing tree...stripped of its voice to stand naked in the center of the dance circle...the center of the universe...stripped of beauty to bear the bodies of the sacred seekers...two great branches left to make it cross-shaped...to bear the bodies dancing on the earth till flesh gives way and final visions tear our souls toward wholeness.

"I was borne beneath the tree, laid on a bed of sage while reins of buffalo hide were attached to flesh-piercing pegs...I was lifted high as the reins were tightened...then I was dropped to swing between earth and heaven...heaven and earth.

"As I dropped I heard a scream of laughter not my own...it came from far galaxies...mocked was I by dark star people...tempting me to cry for help...cry for one to pull upon my legs so that flesh would tear and agony be over.

"I closed my heart's ear to the voices and prayed for sustaining strength from the Great Turtle...I saw him s-l-o-w-l-y moving toward me through the heavens...s-l-o-w-l-y moving toward me...hour after hour as I swayed between earth and heaven.

"The drums beat out a cadence which my body followed...flailing between earth and heaven...while watchers weakened with wonder at the length of time I hung there...I sounded my eagle wing whistle when I had breath to sing it...a hundred whistles answered as word spread round the tepees that one refused assistance to tear the flesh.

"My eye was on the Turtle creeping through the heavens to the center of my soul. At last he reached the sacred tree...crept down to the cross branches...poised there for a moment...and then dropped his body's great weight to the center of my soul. "My breast flesh gave way...tore itself from pegs and reins...I plummeted into the waiting arms of Mother Earth...I was carried to the place of honor for the dancer whose manhood endured...endured in the Spirit...I had tasted the deepest springs of holiness."

As Tony told the tale of bravery and terror, the twin scars glowed like great eyes. He stopped. He was breathing heavily. I cupped a handful of water and dribbled it over him, caressing the cooling liquid across his body. I did the same to myself.

We sat in silence for a long time. I returned the stare of the eyes in the scars. Finally, I could stand it no longer. I burst out, "Tony, am I going to have to go through the pain of a Sun Dance to have deep visions and dance like a man?"

He answered quickly, "No! You've already done your Sun Dance."

I exploded, "No way! I haven't had the flesh of my breasts pierced. I haven't been tied to a sacred tree to dance on Mother Earth or been suspended between her and Grandfather Sky—not even in one of my worst nightmares."

He moved close to me and took my hand in his. He said with quiet urgency, "You have done your own dance of pain. You have hung between heaven and earth when your daddy hung you on the horse-stall wall.

"You have been at the point of despair when he beat you nearly senseless with a shepherd's crook. He smashed your fingers and injured your knee. But most painful of all, he has tried to destroy you inside by making you feel worthless. You've been doing your Sun Dance in small movements every day of your life. To complete your Sun Dance, to dance like a man, you have to discover where the vision of hope is for you."

I was angry. I shot back at him, "You make it sound like my pain was intended—was planned for by God or Jesus or *El Shaddai* or *Wakan Tanka* or whatever else the holy beings get themselves called. If my abuse is part of God's plan, to hell with God!"

The next thing I knew the rest of the icy bucket of water was unceremoniously dumped over my head. He threw the bucket to the ground and grabbed my shoulders hard. The eyes in his wounds glared into mine. I'm sure the eyes in his head were glaring too, but I couldn't see them in the darkness of the sweat lodge.

He shook me as he spoke: "Your abuse comes from the dark star people who inhabit your daddy. It comes from his poor illness-shattered mind. You have a decision to make, young man. You may let the pain destroy you, let it tear up in anger everything you touch within the world. Even if right now you were able to walk away from your daddy's abuse, that anger would follow you.

"On the other hand, you can let the pain lie fallow and walk with your head held high, assured that you have used his darkness for your strengthening.

"That's the choice you have to make, boy, every moment of your life. Sometimes you will make the wrong choice. But the right choice always awaits you.

"The pain of the Sun Dance can never match the pain I feel over my people's destruction. It can never be matched by the pain I feel at the way Indians were portrayed for Wild West Show audiences. Sometimes I make wrong choices when I deal with my pain. You once found me drunk in a straw stack.

"But *Wakan Tanka* never leaves me without possibility. You have become *hunka*, a beloved sharer.

"No matter what your daddy has done to you or will do to you, who you really are cannot be destroyed unless you allow that destruction."

I sat speechless in the dark. I always wanted to feel sorry for myself because of the terror in which I lived. Now, Tony Great Turtle had robbed me of that luxury. I could hold on to my anger no longer.

He began to chant a familiar litany:

Father, Great Spirit, behold this boy!
Your ways shall he see!
Father, Great Spirit, behold this boy!
Your ways shall he see!

Father, Great Spirit, behold this boy!
Your ways shall he see!

My Hermit Uncle John opened the tent flap as though on cue. We staggered out, weak from emotions generated in the cleansing heat. The eastern sky blazed with a shower of falling stars. We had both defeated some dark star people.

Uncle John guided Tony toward the lake. As we reached the edge of the launching rock, Uncle John said quietly, "After caring for the molten rocks, the water would feel kinda' good. I wouldn't mind drowning a few dark star people who took up residence inside me at the Battle of the Marne when all my friends were killed."

He slipped quickly out of his clothes. Together we entered the sacred waters.

When we emerged, my nose was again assailed by the now even more delicious smell of something cooking. We walked up to the coals from the rock fire. Uncle John said without a trace of a stammer, "I hope I didn't do anything that's going to anger your 'spirit friends.' I made double use of the coals. I heated the rocks. I also fixed us a little food.

"We're being overrun with squirrels, so I had a little conversation with Earth Mother. 'Earth Mother,' I said, 'them little varmints is raising Cain with my garden. If I could have your permission, I'd like to cook six of them for three hungry men tonight. The squirrels are young and tender so it would take about two apiece to fill us up.' And Earth Mother said, 'John, they've been keeping the Lazy Susan's awake at night which just makes them lazier. You'd be doing me a favor if you removed a half dozen.'

"Well, having gotten permission from Earth Mother for the squirrels, I begged her pardon for stripping some leaves off the corn stalks. I put the leaves to soak in the lake.

"I shot my squirrels and dressed them out. I stuffed them with black walnuts from the holy tree and with mashed turnips. I wrapped each one in several layers of soaked corn leaves. I nestled them in coals around the rocks. They've been cooking for two hours. They should be about perfect."

Tony removed his sacred deerskin from his medicine bag and spread it on the rock. We sat on our folded clothes. My Hermit Uncle John laid two fragrant packages at each of our places.

Every event can be a learning experience. I learned that squirrel served directly from a fire pit is white hot. I burned my fingers.

Tony smiled in the moonlight. He said, "Perhaps a long prayer might hold back your eagerness and protect you from further damage, Rog."

He rose in the moonlight, his eagle feather in his hand. He faced the east and extended the feather to Grandfather Sky, alive now with a million stars. No falling evil ones were visible.

He chanted:

The light of Wakan Tanka is upon us.
It is making the night world bright.
We are now happy!
All beings that move are rejoicing.
O Mother Earth, be merciful to us!
We eat that we may live.
Our Grandfather, Wakan Tanka,
Give to us a path which is sacred.
Keep us on a path which is sacred.

We dined on sacramental squirrel in the light of the full moon. Having finished the feast, Tony began another chant in Lakota. John picked up the little drum and softly, persistently beat out a contrapuntal rhythm. My clumsy feet began to move. I stepped out on the launching rock and danced, losing myself in the incense of the gifts from Mother Earth, the song, the drum sound and the moonlight. For the first time in my life I felt infinitely graceful. I was dancing like a man.

INTERLUDE 6

The chimes of ten o'clock reverberated through the tiny cabin. I stepped to the living room and put more wood in the potbellied heating stove. My Hermit Uncle John was snoring loudly.

Tony rasped out, "Rog."

I stepped to his side. He was staring straight ahead. It was difficult for him to even move his eyes. His body had become like a dry leaf in autumn ready to drop from its protecting tree. Tony would soon fall fully to earth while his indomitable spirit soared.

I touched his lips with water enabling him to let a few words stumble out:

O Cody!
Longhair Bill Cody!
How many times must you kill my people?
How many times must you kill my heart?

You destroyed something in me at every performance, Bill Cody...you killed something of my manhood...something of my people's beauty. Hetchetu welo!

You seemed invincible, riding in the spotlight...you would ride forever...leaving us forever broken.

And yet you were broken...lost your fortune...cheated by your crafty partners...even lost your chosen grave site...you were upstaged by the world.

You died a broken man in Denver...January 17, 1917...yet the world mourned your loss...the dealer in fantasy who took people to a world that never was...making us out a people who never really were as you portrayed us.

The staged killings you forced upon us we did in desperation...the heart of our freedom and our Mother Earth religion was torn out nightly and twice on Saturdays...you killed some-

thing in my people by planting in the minds of others our essential worthlessness.

Yet you too died, Bill Cody...died in degradation...died a broken old man...when I heard the news, I wept...wept for the passing of a time and of a people...wept for your passing, Longhair Bill Cody...wept for the passing of Pehaska...wept for the passing of one who meant well.

Can our people rise again...can brokenness be healed and the sacred rediscovered...that sacred which was lost in your extravaganza?

It can only be restored if I start with my dying moment: I must forgive you, Bill Cody. Earth Mother demands that I forgive you. I do forgive you. Hetchetu welo.

O Cody!
Longhair Bill Cody!
Generations have passed
And I must forgive you.
I do forgive you.

Tony Great Turtle sobbed weakly. I gathered him into my arms and held him close.

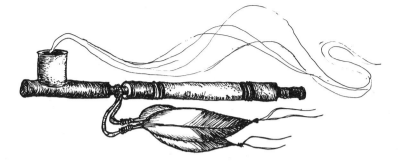

THE CROSS AND THE
ABALONE SHELL

The huge vacant lot next to the Skelly gas station was guarded by
an enormous flying red horse shaped into the station's sign. I
would often stare into the great stallion's eye, longing to be
carried away into the sky on his mythic back and float forever
among the distant constellations.

Once I was sure he winked at me. That night in my dream I
rode away on his back to Greece. He stabled himself in pillared
temple ruins above the Aegean Sea, while I lived happily ever-
after munching grapes and goat cheese.

The lot was the site for all kinds of entertainments that roamed
the countryside. Professor Grisham's Traveling Herbal Emporium would come to cure our bodies. Blind Ben See's Carnival
of Wonders would pass through, astounding our imaginations.
The lady evangelist, Helen Jepson, would pause to save our souls.

They were always intertwined in my mind. Tony Great Turtle
had told me about finding refuge with each of them at one time
or another. I never learned what he was running away from. I
never asked. I was just glad he kept appearing at special moments to help me live beyond my pain.

Just after Father MacCarrity arrived as priest at St. Ignatius
the Lesser Roman Catholic Church (shortened to "St. Iggie's"
by most the residents of Pheasant Valley), word arrived from
nearby Pleasant Plain that Helen Jepson was going to make our

town the next stop on her evangelistic circuit. Father MacCarrity was furious that the inhabitants of his parish would be subjected to a woman preaching the Gospel. After all, hadn't St. Paul himself forbidden such heretical activity? Father MacCarrity could threaten his parishioners with divine retribution if they *attended* the meetings, but it was a little hard to prevent them from *hearing* the blasphemous goings-on. Miss Helen barely broke five feet tall, but she had a voice that was truly miraculous. She could be heard all over town without the aid of a loudspeaker.

I first met Miss Helen under less than auspicious circumstances. Three years earlier Pheasant Valley had been graced by a real-live circus. When Mom and Dad and I had gone in for Saturday-night shopping, I slipped away to the big top and crawled under a flap. I had an instantaneous glimpse of paradise: music and animals and human bodies flying through the air. I lay on the crushed grass, absolutely enraptured. Then I saw a security guard bearing down on me, and I slithered back out the way I'd come in.

The following week when we returned to town there was another tent set up. Through the ensuing days, images from my brief encounter with the circus formed the framework of my dreams. Hopelessly earthbound to pain in real life, I floated from trapeze to trapeze while the spectators wildly applauded my valor.

I decided I'd take a look at this new show. It was early evening and no crowd had arrived. I stealthily slipped around to the rear of the tent, flopped on my belly and began to wiggle my way under the worn canvas.

I was stopped by the iron grasp of two hands on my disappearing ankles. The image of a security guard flashed across my mind as did the bars on the jail window where I would surely be incarcerated for my transgressions.

I was slowly, unceremoniously pulled backward, eating dirt like the serpent cast out from Eden. When my head cleared the tent base, I kicked free, leaped to my feet and prepared to flee.

I was stopped by the sparkling eyes, wide grin and open arms of a woman several inches shorter than I. In a voice that reflected both an edge of thunder's rumble and the soft rush of April wind, she said, "Boy, you don't have to creep under a tent flap to get into the kingdom of God. You can always come in through the door."

She paused for a moment to let her words register in my startled brain. She continued. "Now, I think you'd better tell me what your name is."

I responded hesitantly, "R-R-Rog."

She put an arm around me. "Well, Rog, my name is Helen Jepson. You can call me Miss Helen. Most folks do. Now you come on inside. I need some help arranging the chairs before people come to hear the stories."

I was puzzled and asked, "St-Stories? I d-d-didn't know you w-were a st-st-storyteller. I heard t-tell that you were some s-s-sort of p-p-preacher lady."

She laughed. "That's what I do mostly: tell stories. But then, that's mostly what God does too: tells stories in mountains, and storms, and sunlight and people. He told the finest, scariest, happiest, most saving story of all when he walked, and walks, among us in his son, Jesus Christ."

I looked at her in amazement. She sounded exactly like Gletha, the goatlady.

Miss Helen took me inside the canvas kingdom of God— through the door.

I looked up. A huge, rough-hewn cross was suspended from the tent peak. A gaunt face, two hands and two feet had been fastened to one side of the cross in the proper places. They looked as if they had been cut out of brown wrapping paper. As the strange object rotated in the air currents, I got the eerie feeling that the cross was both empty and full.

On one of its rotations I noticed that wasps flying in and out of a crack in the canvas had started to build a nest on the cross figure's brown-paper forehead. From a distance it looked like they were shaping a crown of thorns.

I hoped the cross was securely fastened up there. My daddy was always saying I had to be hit in the head to learn anything. I hoped the risen figure wouldn't have to go that far in my instruction.

What a storyteller Miss Helen turned out to be! I learned about Hosea who married a whore and Jeremiah thrown down a well, and Peter and James and John who followed the wandering teacher. She took Jesus out of stained-glass windows, dirtied his feet in the dust of Palestine, made him a sweat and flesh and blood man, and then blazed his resurrected Spirit into her listeners' hearts. I was spellbound.

I never missed a chance to hear her preach. I was surprised when I first discovered that Tony Great Turtle had traveled with her as her roustabout for short periods of time. He was in charge of putting up the tent.

Now she was returning to Pheasant Valley, not knowing that she faced a formidable opponent in Father MacCarrity. He decided to strategize a plan of action. On the first night of the services parish leaders would gather on the spacious screened-in front porch of Heinrich and Eva Dummler right across the street from the tent. They would listen to the enemy and then see if they could strike a deal with the city fathers to close her down on some pretext or other.

It was rumored that Heinrich Dummler made the best home brew in the county. The onerous task of censorship would be sweetened a bit.

That first night Miss Helen was at her best. She held the folk in the packed tent and the folk on the porch absolutely spellbound. She wove together the story of Ruth, a foreign woman who became an ancestor of Jesus, and the parable of the Good Samaritan. She made a plea for folk to not look down on other folk, pointing out that Jesus himself came from foreign stock and that an outcast Samaritan had saved a battered man. She made me think of Tony's stories of his people suffering at the hands of so-called Christians.

Miss Helen announced that there would be no special invitation for folk to commit their lives to Jesus. She wanted them to come back all three nights to get the whole story. Anybody who committed to Jesus had better *really* know what they were doing.

There were tears of joy in the tent and grudging approval on the porch. Even Father MacCarrity had to admit that much of what was said made sense even if it came from the forbidden mouth of a preaching woman. The decision was made that the committee would return the following night. Surely she would slip into some heresy which would merit her being closed down and driven out of town.

On the following evening not only was the tent packed but the Dummler's porch overflowed with people down the steps and onto the front yard. Eva Dummler was dumbfounded at how many folks from the parish decided to "just drop by for a minute." Heinrich closed his cellar so as not to use up his entire season's supply of golden brew.

Miss Helen deepened her plea for compassion and understanding, for living out the love of Jesus who loved us so much he died on a cross and rose so he could continue to teach and love through us. The lovers from the *Song of Songs* and faithful Stephen and tormented Paul were woven through her drama of God's caring for creation. It sounded like Tony's concern for Mother Earth.

Again there were tears and hugs in tent and yard and porch. Father MacCarrity was even more charitable—but feared she was "leading up to something."

The next morning I got a ride into town with neighbors and headed for her van in which she lived while she was on the road. Miss Helen greeted me warmly and said she hoped I could come back that evening: "After the meeting tonight I'm going to serve the Supper of the Lord to the folk who come forward. I could use your help."

I exploded, "I'll b-b-bet you c-c-can use my h-h-help. We m-m-may be servin' s-supper to a l-l-lot of f-folk. We'll b-be fryin' chicken all d-day!"

Her laugh rippled out. She explained how forgetful people needed a reminder of what Jesus had done for them. So she would have them dip bread in grape juice. Then I remembered. Years before, I'd had the Supper with Otto Wickhorst just before he died. He'd had me say special words about "This is my body" and "This is my blood." We'd used the fluted crust from an apple pie and strong black coffee as our reminders.

I asked, "Do you have bread for the Supper? My Hermit Uncle John bakes the best bread in Sunrise Township. I know he'd be glad to share. He's real good at that."

She was delighted with the proposed gift. I asked her what I was supposed to do tonight. She took out a large box, and we walked together to the tent. She placed the box on the table in the front and removed the newspaper-wrapped contents.

She said, "When one is dealing with the Lord, one should give unto Him the best that one has."

She unwrapped a large gold-rimmed plate resplendent with rosebuds. She explained, "I got this as a premium with a fifty pound bag of flour years ago. There's a song about Jesus sung at Christmas: 'Lo, How a Rose E're Blooming.'"

She then removed the largest, most ornate mustache cup I'd ever seen. Tiny cherubs danced upon its gold-flecked sides. She continued, "This is the only thing I took away when my father died. I always imagined that it was little angels such as these who sang Jesus to sleep in the Bethlehem manger."

Her laugh floated out again. "At least that makes a good story. Tonight I want you to stand by my side and hold the plate of bread. Folk will break off a piece and dip it in the cup. Now why don't you run to your uncle's and see if we really can have some of his fine bread."

I did as I was told. My Uncle John was delighted to have his bread used in acting out the Last Supper. Before he let me leave he sat me down and read me the story from his worn Bible, saying, "This is how Luke reports the Holy Meal. Each Gospel story about it is a little different. Don't worry about that. No four people would ever see an event quite the same way. Listen:

And when the hour was come, he sat down, and the twelve apostles with him. And he took bread, and gave thanks and brake it, and gave unto them, saying, 'This is my body which is given for you: this do in remembrance of me.' Likewise also the cup after supper, saying, 'This cup is the new testament in my blood, which is shed for you.'"

When I delivered Uncle John's beautiful brown loaf, Miss Helen praised it as a perfect offering to Jesus.

That night the crowd gathered in tent, yard and porch. There was a sense of eager anticipation. Miss Helen focused entirely on Jesus. He snuggled children and healed lepers and broke rules right and left to establish a new rule of love. He annoyed so many folk that they tried to kill him, but you can't defeat either God or God's Son.

Then she paused and invited folk to turn their lives around and try to live and love like that Jesus. About thirty people came forward and knelt on the crushed grass. Miss Helen moved down the line and prayed a moment with each of them, her hands on their heads.

She invited these special seekers to rise to new life. She asked them to stay after the meeting because she wanted to spend some moments just with them as she shared a special story.

She thanked the rest of the folk for coming, assured them that she'd be back next year, and then closed with, "I have only one request. Even if you did not come forward, live your lives as if you had."

The crowd dispersed from tent and yard and porch. When everyone was gone except Father MacCarrity, Heinrich Dummler re-opened his cellar and brought up two huge tankards of his fine brew.

Father Mac's charitable mood deepened as his tankard emptied. He had to admit that he found little to fault in the storyteller across the street. He and Heinrich didn't pay much attention to further activities beneath the canvas until Miss Helen spoke the fateful words to those who had come forward: "We're forgetful people. We need to be reminded of just what Christ did for us and what we must do for Christ: be his flesh and blood in the world. We're going to celebrate the Supper of Our Lord."

Father Mac choked on his beer. He leaped to his feet without a word, shot through the screen door and across the street like a human cannonball in a circus act, and stormed into the tent, shouting: "You will not. No woman's voice can speak the sacred words. No woman's hands will touch my Lord's Body and Blood and make a mockery of the sacrament."

His breath was coming in short, angry gasps. He raised his arm as if he would sweep cup and plate from the table. I had just stepped to Miss Helen's side. I was scared to death. People cowered in the front chairs before the onslaught of this black-robed cyclone.

Miss Helen did not cower. She turned serenely, placed a hand on his shaking arm and caught his raging eye in a steady gaze. She said in a low voice, "Father MacCarrity: yesterday was Sunday. I did not come raging into St. Ignatius. I respect the way you tell your story. I only ask the same from you.

"You say no woman's voice should speak the holy words. Yet was it not a woman's voice that first proclaimed the message entrusted at the Resurrection? Was it not a woman's voice that sang lullabies to the Holy Child and mourned with his torn body in her arms? You say a woman's hands should never touch bread and cup. Look at my hands. It was hands like these with which Mary changed and cherished the Holy Babe. It was with hands like these that Veronica wiped the blood and sweat from our Lord's brow on the Via Dolorosa. Yes, I know and love that story. It was hands like these that Magdalene used to anoint the Master's feet.

"Dear Father—yes, I'll grace you with that title of respect—dear Father MacCarrity..."

Her voice took on an edge of passion as she continued, "Don't ever tell me that hands like these are not worthy to touch common bread and juice made holy in human flesh."

As she spoke, he backed away. He sat in the shadows at the

rear of the tent.

Miss Helen read the same story from the Bible that Hermit Uncle John had read to me. She talked about what it really meant to carry the body and blood of Jesus within us—what it should mean in the world when we left the tent.

One by one the people stepped forward, broke off a piece of the splendid bread, dipped it in the cup which Miss Helen held in one hand while she hugged them with her free arm. They slipped away in the darkness to hopefully turn their lives around beyond the tent.

When everyone had left, Miss Helen stood for a long moment looking at Father MacCarrity still sitting in the shadows. Then, motioning for me to follow, she headed down the center aisle. We stepped before the silent man. He rose.

There was only a small morsel of bread and a few crumbs left on the plate. Some folk not accustomed to ecclesiastical nicety had liked the bread so much that they came back for a second piece. I held the plate. He took the bread, dipped it in the juice and placed it in his mouth.

He looked at Miss Helen for a long moment. Taking the moustache cup gently from her hand, he raised it to his lips and drained it. The ceramic bridge protected his snow white moustache from stain. His free-flowing tears leavened the holy liquid.

Continuing to hold the cup, he reached beneath his robes and pulled out a neatly pressed snow-white handkerchief. He shook it open and carefully dried the inside of the strange chalice. As he removed the handkerchief in the half-light of the tent, the grape juice on the fabric resembled the face of Christ in the stained-glass window.

He took the plate and carefully brushed the crumbs into the handkerchief which he had stretched over the palm of his left hand. He handed me back the plate and reverently folded the crumbs into the once snow-white cloth.

He said, "I shall place this in the tabernacle at St. Ignatius."

He disappeared into the darkness.

I didn't know what his last words meant. Miss Helen must have understood. Her cheeks were diamonded with tears.

It was to Helen Jepson that Tony Great Turtle turned the last time I saw him before Uncle John and I found him beneath the great black walnut tree. It seemed to me the eighty-seven-year-old man was getting more and more frail. We never knew quite where he went when he disappeared. We only knew that we rejoiced when he came again.

Miss Helen was in Pheasant Valley during one of his strange appearances. I had headed to my Hermit Uncle John's to fish for bullheads. I was careful to catch only what our family could eat. Tony had taught me that lesson forever.

I sat on the shore for over an hour without a single bite. The mud turtles were not even stealing the worms from my often-checked hook.

All of a sudden I heard the sound of his rainstick. I turned to greet him. At that moment my throw line burned through my hands. I quickly stomped down on it with my foot.

I began to pull in the heavy fish, carefully coiling my line on the rock. Tony stepped to my side. Our images were reflected together in the lake.

The fish swam into the floating image of Tony. It lay quietly in the water as if mesmerized. I saw that it was not a lowly bullhead which I usually caught, but a huge bass. As I raised it to the rock, I knew it would provide dinner for three of us.

Not needing to fish anymore, I decided to quiz Tony. I always liked to talk to him. For one thing, I seldom stammered in his presence. "Tony, Miss Helen says that once in a while you travel with her to help her set up her tent. Does that mean you're a Christian."

He looked at me strangely. "Miss Helen is a fine person. I sometimes set up her tent and take it down—and disappear in between. I seldom hear her preach. She doesn't try to convert me. She's always told me that I'm a good man. She's paid me well. She understands that I can't live inside a name. I am a shaman. My great-grandmother taught me to look beneath names to the spirit from which word shadows grow. I must always try to find ways of healing the world which we humans have torn. I must always try to weave the wisdom of the upper world and the lower world into this world, or all living things will die.

"She's said I should use my visions and my ceremonies to make of myself a hole through which the power of understanding will come to the two-leggeds."

I interrupted. "But, Tony, Pastor Phitz at the Baptist Church of Peter-the-Rock is always telling the congregation if they don't take Jesus Christ as their personal savior, they'll rot in hell. Sometimes you can hear him shouting clear across the lake."

Tony had a faraway look on his face as he stared out over the water. He murmured, "The record of good *wasichu* Christians and their dealings with my people is salted with our tears. From the beginning, too many good Christians who made covered wagon ruts over Mother Earth's belly and laced her with iron rails looked upon us as filthy vermin to be destroyed. I want you to read something, Rog, so you'll really understand how the children of *Wakan Tanka* were seen."

He pulled an envelope from his leather bag. It contained the title page of a book and a second loose page. There was a picture of the author, a smiling evangelist named Duke Davis. His work was called *Flashlights from Mountain and Plain*. The Pentecostal Union had released it in 1911. Tony had underlined some sentences:

> We look upon the Indian in his primitive state, and we marvel at his savage nature, and his apparent low aim in life...
>
> With a thirst for blood and a gluttonous appetite for the wild meats of the forest, he seems content to live and fight, and hunt and die with the hope of going to a happy hunting ground upon parting this life...
>
> His idea of a home life reaches no higher than a tepee...
>
> If he could have really developed the habit of call-

ing on the Lord, it might have helped the Indian raise his standard of life...

Generally speaking, an Indian is an Indian and for a man to make anything else of him is a hard task. He will go back to his old evil ways even after cultural opportunities.

I was heavyhearted as I finished reading. I saw the terrible pain in Tony's aging face. As he put the worn, yellowing envelope back in his bag, Tony murmured, "It was good Christians who made a treaty with Chief Red Cloud in 1868 when I was eleven years old. They assured us that our most sacred lands, the *Paha Sapa*, what you call the Black Hills, would always be ours as long as the grass should grow and the waters flow.

"Eight winters later, soldiers under chief scout Longhair Bill Cody were driving us away. Some of our people were lured to the *wasichu* forts. Some of our chiefs were carried off alone and were forced to put marks on treaty papers which allowed the land to be sold. Maybe they were crazy from drinking *minne wakan*, white man's whiskey. I know about that craziness."

He began to sob. "Only crazy men or very foolish men would sell Mother Earth."

I rubbed his back. I wanted somehow to distract him from his sadness.

An idea suddenly occurred to me: "Tony, I was going to see Miss Helen this afternoon. Why don't you come along? I know she'd like to see you."

He stared out over the holy lake for a long moment as if waiting for a message from his spirit world. His hands moved the rainstick in a particular pattern. Voices murmured within it. Had "friends" from the rock been summoned to advise the sad old man? Then he said, "I must see her one last time."

I retrieved my fish. He picked up his bag. I took his arm to steady him as we made our way over the rough path to the cabin of my Hermit Uncle John.

Uncle John admired my catch and put it in his battered ice box. I wheedled him into driving us to Pheasant Valley. I wasn't sure Tony could endure the long walk through the fields. Uncle John wrapped a loaf of bread in wax paper "just in case Miss Helen might enjoy it."

We arrived at Miss Helen's evangelistic site. A brief shower had broken the August heat and washed the dust from the world. Her tent glowed golden under the benevolent stare of the mythological red horse.

Uncle John let us out and drove on down Main Street to buy groceries at the Red Owl store.

We could hear Miss Helen inside neatening things up for her final evening service. I decided for old-times sake that I would crawl under the tent flap and scare the daylights out of her.

Tony paused, the loaf of bread in one hand and his bag in the other, grinning at my prank. I began to slither under. I did not realize that Miss Helen had simultaneously stepped outside through the front door. I was almost inside.

Suddenly my heels were again grasped. I was summarily extricated as I'd been the first time. Four hands began tickling me all over. I collapsed in helpless giggles.

They pulled me to my feet and, muddy as I was, we had a three-way hug laced together by free-floating laughter.

Miss Helen advised that I go baptize myself with the hose on the side of the gas station to remove the mud. She picked up the bread which had been resting on Tony's bag. They stepped into the tent.

I dawdled at my cleansing task. I squirted the horse. Did his feathered wings fluff out a bit in pleasure? Suddenly Bert McKay who owned the station yelled at me to stop horsing around. He was grinning as he yelled. I waved, turned off the hose and entered the tent.

Tony and Miss Helen were in deep conversation. The table had been transformed. Tony's sacred deerskin now covered it. The cup and plate graced by the golden loaf glowed in the soft mysterious light which filtered through the canvas. Between them was Tony Great Turtle's abalone shell containing sacred herbs ready for the fire. The rough wooden cross suspended from the tent peak turned slowly in the air currents.

I blurted out, "Wow! I didn't know all the ceremonies we've been doing with the abalone shell were really Christian."

Tony winced. Miss Helen put a protective hand on his arm. She said quietly, "They're not. But that does not mean Tony's ceremonies are wrong. They are one path of light through the darkness."

I was still confused. "But how come you as a Christian let Tony travel with you sometimes and help with your tent without converting him first. I thought Christians by and large saw Indians as dirty, filthy pagans."

She spoke to me sharply: "Don't ever let yourself become a part of the 'by and large.' You'll hurt people terribly and sometimes close your eyes to a path toward hope.

"Tony and I have discovered we have a special bond. Tony's aging parents were massacred at Wounded Knee. My father was a soldier who rode up with reinforcements after the killing was finally halted."

They both had tears in their eyes. I didn't understand anything about Wounded Knee. I knew all about Custer's last stand because he was one of my daddy's heroes. A line I often heard from him played in my head: "The killing of Custer and his men was another act of murder by those damn worthless Sioux Indians."

Now I was beginning to see another side of history.

Tony stared up at the cross turning in the breeze. He began to story-chant: "Missionaries of Mormons, of Adventists, of Methodists and Catholics told our people of a Messiah's Second Coming. Some *wasichus* stood white-robed in cemeteries, waiting to be taken up to heaven. Wovoka from the Paiute tribe, hearing all the stories, received a special vision from *Wakan Tanka*. He saw himself as the Messiah bringing hope to all of us. He set the people dancing the Spirit Dance, the Ghost Dance. In his vision *wasichus* would disappear. Buffalo would run again. Indians killed by *wasichus* would walk the earth once more.

"All over the country Indians danced the Ghost Dance: starving people on reservations, fugitives in canyons all danced in painted shirts which bullets could not enter—or so the vision went.

"The president and farmers, generals and governors all feared the dancers, knowing that lying savages would surely rape and kill. Chief Big Foot and three hundred seventy followers were surrounded by four hundred seventy soldiers on the creek called Wounded Knee.

"The *wasichu* opened fire in the great confusion. Some of their bullets slaughtered thirty-one of their own men. Warriors and women, children and the aged bloodied the snow. Three hundred Indians were cast into a common grave. I never saw my parents' bodies to do the proper prayers."

Tony addressed the figure who seemed in sunlight and shadow to be weeping on the cross. "Savior of the *wasichus*, do not try to come again if you only bring destruction—destruction to my people. Do not come again."

A great wail seemed torn from his heart. Then he sobbed silently.

Miss Helen stepped to him, placed a hand on his shoulder and said, "The problem isn't the Savior coming. It's the people listening. Maybe it wouldn't be a bad idea if we started with ourselves—if we prepared ourselves to listen. It might be especially good for the boy."

My defenses went up immediately. My dad was always trying to teach me to listen by inflicting pain on me. My wrists began to itch, not only from remembering the time when my daddy hung me on the barn wall with the new hemp rope, but in anticipation of one way Tony and Miss Helen might be contemplating making me listen.

Once Tony and I had waded into the holy lake for one of his special rituals. Afterwards, we were sitting on the launching rock, letting the warm breeze dry us, when I noticed the scars on the undersides of his wrists. I asked him how he'd gotten them. It looked as if he'd been gnawed by some kind of animal.

He had laughed wryly and said, "I could tell you a story about how I wrestled with a bear in a cave but that wouldn't be true. The scars were burned there when I was a boy being trained to endure great pain and to focus on *Wakan Tanka*'s voice speaking in my heart. My shaman great-grandmother lighted sunflower seeds afire in her sacred abalone shell. Then she took the tip of a knife and transferred the burning seeds to my wrists. If I was truly meant to listen as a holy one, I would not wince or drop the seeds. I didn't wince."

I quickly glanced at the abalone shell to see if there were any seeds in it. There were not. I was somewhat reassured that a different technique was about to be employed enabling me to listen to the sacred.

Tony struck a match and lighted the herbs in the shell. He fanned them with the feather from his hat. A rich smudge arose. He offered the smoke to the four directions, then to Grandfather Sky and to Mother Earth.

He elevated the shell, raised his right hand with the index finger pointed straight up and chanted:

Grandfather, I send my voice to you.
Grandfather, I send my voice to you.
With all the universe I send my voice to you,
That we may live.

I looked up. The cross was bathed with smoke. Wasps were fleeing through the crack in the tent top. When the paper-sack face appeared, it seemed to be wearing a broad grin.

My Hermit Uncle John had read me stories from the Old Testament. Yahweh God or *El Shaddai* or the Holy One, or whichever name the folk at a particular time called their God, enjoyed the smell of good plump sheep and goats offered with a little extra fat thrown in.

In the half-light and shadows the smiling Jesus seemed to like the rich aroma of sage and sweet grass as much as I did. I might someday believe in a Jesus like that.

Tony smudged himself and each of us in turn. I was fascinated that his movement followed the pattern of a cross.

Miss Helen stepped to the table. She picked up the rose plate with the bread and elevated it the same way that Tony had lifted the shell. She said, "Come, let us receive the Supper of the Lord. Hear the words of Holy Scripture:

> And he took bread, and gave thanks, and brake it, and gave unto them, saying, 'This is my body which is given for you: this do in remembrance of me.'"

She set the plate down and elevated the mustache cup. She continued: "After the supper Jesus took the cup, saying,

> 'This cup is the new testament in my blood, which is shed for you.'"

We each broke off a piece of bread, dipped it in the cup and savored the goodness of the wheat underscored by the tang of pure grape juice.

I became aware of a strange humming sound. At first I thought the wasps were returning with a swarm of angry friends. Then I realized the sound was coming from Tony. It deepened. Lakota words emerged from the flow. I did not understand any of them.

There was no movement in the tent. The cross had stopped rotating. Tony and the Christ were staring deeply into each other's eyes.

Miss Helen watched without moving. She motioned me to step in front of Tony. He turned his gaze on me. He said in the very voice of the Thunderbird, "I have been granted a vision by *Wakan Tanka*. It is a vision of your name. You must receive a new inner name."

I protested, "But I like my name. I like Rog or Roger. I used to hate it when Gletha called me Rogee. But she says now I've grown into my real name. I'm not sure I can bear the weight of another one."

Tony responded sharply, "You have no choice. I am a hole into the fabric of the beyond. Your name has slipped through to me. It wants to rest within you. You must receive it now or it will be lost."

I looked helplessly at Miss Helen. A half smile played on her lips. I finally acquiesced.

Tony reached into his bag and placed his eaglebone whistle on the table's edge. He removed the sacred pipe, assembled it as he spoke the familiar ceremony, smudged it and offered it to the six directions. He lighted the *kinnikinnik*, inhaled smoke and handed the pipe to Miss Helen who chastely sniffed a bit of smoke rising from the pipe bowl.

Tony reached into his bag and removed the pouch of sage gathered in a sacred manner. He drew Miss Helen close to the two of us. He scattered sage on the ground in a perfect circle. He said, "We now dwell for a moment in the sacred hoop. Here the universe is centered. Here the name will be revealed."

He took the pipe, raised it and sang the *Cannumpa wakan oloowan*, the sacred pipe song:

Friend, do this! Friend, do this! Friend, do this!
If you do this, your Grandfather will see you.
When you stand within the holy circle,
Think of me when you place the sacred tobacco
in the pipe.
If you do this, He will give you all that you ask for.
Friend, do this! Friend, do this! Friend, do this!
If you do this, your Grandfather will see you.
When you stand within the holy circle,
Send your voice to Wakan Tanka.
If you do this, he will give you all that you desire.
Friend, do this! Friend, do this! Friend, do this!
If you do this, your Grandfather will see you.
When you stand within the holy circle,
Crying and with tears,
Send your voice to Wakan Tanka.
If you do this, you will have all that you desire.
Friend, do this! Friend, do this! Friend, do this!
That your Grandfather may see you.
When you stand within the sacred hoop,
Raise your hand to Wakan Tanka.
Do this and he will bestow upon you all that you desire.

Tony placed the pipe on the table so that the stem rested on the bread plate and the bowl leaned against the cup. During the pipe song Miss Helen had noticed the smudge dying out. She took the feather which was still lying on the table, fanned the fire into life and returned the feather to its resting place.

Tony put his hand on my left shoulder. I felt a shock of power which vibrated through my body as if I had touched a live electric fence. He motioned for me to pick up the eagle feather in my right hand and extend it upwards. I felt my hand drawn toward the cross. Miss Helen put her hand on my right shoulder.

Lakota words flowed out from Tony. A phrase was repeated over and over again. It shaped itself into three repetitions in English:

Father, Great Spirit, behold this boy.
Your ways may he see.

The chant quickened:

My Grandfather, the sun, you who walk yellow,
Look down on us, look down on us.
Pity us. Pity us.
May this young man facing straight
Be helped to walk for his life!
Those that shine above at night,
And the animals of the night,
We pray to you.
The morning star and my father, listen.
I have asked for long breath, for large life.
May this young man, with his people and his relatives,
Do well, walking where it is good,
Obtaining food and clothing and
Horses of many colors,
And where there are birds that are crying and
The day is long and the wind is good!
Animals that move on the surface,
Animals under ground that inhabit the water,
Listen, be attentive.
This one standing here asks of you a name that is good.

Tony picked up the eaglebone whistle and gave three haunting, shrill-toned blasts upon it. The sound sent chills through my body. The pull on my hand made me feel on the edge of levitation. I was very light-headed.

Tony began a final chant:

> *Morning star, affirm his inner name:*
> *Hope-bringer.*
> *Grandfather sun,*
> *Burn the meaning of his name in his heart:*
> *Hope-bringer.*
> *Spirits of the stones,*
> *Lighten his steps as he lives out his name:*
> *Hope-bringer.*
> *Great Turtle, my guardian,*
> *Carry him through the dark star people as*
> *Hope-bringer.*

He gave three further blasts on the eaglebone whistle. My hand was released from the mysterious power. It fell to my side. I nearly collapsed on the beaten ground. I turned to the table and drained the mustache cup. The rich smell of sage, sweet grass and bread were woven into the sharp taste of the juice. I was supposed to walk out of the tent a different person, a real hope-bringer.

I looked up once more to the smiling Christ. There seemed to be another figure hanging there. Then I saw that it was me, suspended by ropes against the wall of the horse stall. My daddy stood there cursing the worthlessness of his naked son. For only a moment my anger flared in its customary fashion. Then I found myself whispering words in unison with the figure on the cross: "Father, forgive him. He doesn't know what he's doing."

I understood for the first time what my new name really meant.

EPILOGUE

The ancient grandfather's clock chimed eleven. The storm whispered to an end.

The old shaman lay quiet. Sweat ran from every crevice in his ancient face. A damp stain spread on the pillow beneath his head.

My Hermit Uncle John appeared at my shoulder. He murmured, "Death stalks gently."

Tony slowly turned his head toward us. He rasped out haltingly, "It's time to begin our journey to Shaman's Point."

We removed the mustard plaster and wrapped his gnarled body in his sacred deerskin. We surrounded him with his worn ground-length black greatcoat. I balanced his leather hat with the eagle feather over his brow. He smiled.

I placed his leather medicine bag in his trembling hands. He caressed it.

We carried him carefully through the cabin. His breath came easier for a moment and he asked, "Would you place me in John's great chair? I want to talk with Thunderbird."

A kerosene wall lamp burned above the image which Uncle John had shaped in arrowheads on the wall mat. Its eyes blazed as the old man looked deeply into them. He requested, "Cut a corner from my deerskin. Cut the end from my right braid. Wrap the hair in the skin and place it on the table beneath Thunderbird. Something of my spirit will remain here as a blessing."

We did as he requested while he sang haltingly:

Because my spirit joins the Spirit
in all created things,
May you remember every moment in this lodge
that each step you take upon Mother Earth
should be as a prayer.
Your eyes are wakan:
see all things and all people in a wakan manner,
Your mouth is wakan: each word you say should
reflect your holy state in this place
and every place.
Since you are now soul-keepers,
you must never be in conflict.
You are fully wakan.
Remain in peace forever.

Tony made one last request of his friend: "John, bring the drum."

Uncle John picked up the little drum from beneath Thunderbird and threaded its loop onto the belt of his sheepskin coat.

We picked Tony up carefully. He weighed little more than the summer scarecrow we mounted to frighten the blackbirds from the gooseberries.

We carried him up the narrow path to the tip of Shaman's Point. Holding him, I sat on the stone bench so the old man could see out over Lake Sumach, the holy lake. Stars danced in the full moon's light.

Tears froze on my cheeks. Tony shuddered deep into my embrace and began to sob. I removed the eagle feather from his leather hat and brushed the tears away before they crystallized.

Behind us, my Hermit Uncle John crouched by the ancient fire pit carved in the rock. I did not hear a match strike before the mysterious red flames leaped to illumine our strange trio.

On the opposite stone bluff across a narrow inlet, voices sang the closing phrases of the Christmas Eve midnight service at the Baptist Church of Peter-the-Rock: "Sleep in heavenly peace. Sleep in heavenly peace." It seemed exactly right that the voices on Shaman's Point joined the Christian benediction.

We waited statue-like for *Wakan Tanka* to move us toward the next step on our sacred journey. The One who surprised the world in a stabled Babe would surely surprise us who waited faithfully. We were caught in an occasional headlight from a departing car.

As the church darkened the silent night returned. Tony whispered, "They've sung their song. It's almost time for you to sing our song to me."

Again his face was wet with sweat. He continued, "Before you do, reach into my medicine bag and pull out the envelope you gave me long ago."

I removed the worn envelope containing the red powder from the sacred turtle smashed by my daddy. Tony instructed me: "On my right cheek outline the sacred turtle which carried me through both stars and eighty-seven years of life."

Uncle John began a steady rhythm on the small drum.

Tony's sweat held the fine powder as I sketched the turtle. It glowed in the firelight. He gave me a final instruction: "On my left cheek sketch a cross. I have tried and failed and tried and succeeded in bringing all appearances of *Wakan Tanka* together. The two of you and Miss Helen have helped me do that. The turtle and the cross must always be together in love."

As I marked him with the sign, the brown paper face, hands and feet from Miss Helen's cross faded into my mind's eye against the steeple which crested Peter-the-Rock. The Christ was smiling.

The old shaman closed his eyes. My voice broke as I sang:

> *Happy journey to you.*
> *Happy journey to you.*
> *Happy journey, dear Tony.*
> *Happy journey to you.*

As he shuddered close against me, Tony Great Turtle died in my arms. The drumbeat stopped.

The voices of our spirit "friends" on Shaman's Point hymned a welcome.

A BIBLIOGRAPHIC NOTE TO READERS

One of the great joys of writing *Tales of Tony Great Turtle* was the opportunity to read widely in Lakota history and spirituality as well as trying to "get inside" Bill Cody. It helped to flesh out childhood images, shadows and stories. Here are some places I explored. I hope the reading of the *Tales* will encourage you to explore as well.

I have attempted to balance historic facts and integrity toward traditions I cherish while retaining the storyteller's freedom to underscore universal truths at the heart of human reality with the tools of imagination.

I did the final editing of this volume with the words of "Declaration of War Against Exploiters of Lakota Spirituality" echoing in my consciousness. This document, ratified by the Dakota, Lakota and Nakota Nations, June, 1993 can be found in Ward Churchill's *Indians are Us?: Culture and Genocide in Native North America*, pp. 273-277.

These tales in no way purport to paint me as an expert in any tradition of Native American Spirituality. They are gifts of thanks to an old man—whoever he really was—who, along with Gletha, the goatlady, and my Hermit Uncle John, saved me spiritually and physically from the ravages of catastrophic childhood abuse. His images and wisdom have become a part of that eclectic world of the Spirit which sustains me today.

LAKOTA BIBLIOGRAPHY

Anderson, Gary Clayton and Woolworth, Alan R., eds. *Through Dakota Eyes: Narrative Accounts of the Minnesota Indian War of 1862*. St. Paul: Minnesota Historical Society Press, 1988.

Bierhorst, John, ed. *The Red Swan: Myths and Tales of the American Indians*. New York: Farrar, Straus and Giroux, 1976.

Bierhorst, John, ed. *The Sacred Path: Spells, Prayers, and Power Songs of the American Indians*. New York: William Morrow and Company, 1983.

Black Elk, Wallace and William S. Lyon. *Black Elk: The Sacred Ways of a Lakota*. San Francisco: Harper, 1990.

Brown, Joseph Epes, recorder and ed. *The Sacred Pipe: Black Elk's Account of the Seven Rites of the Oglala Sioux*. Norman, Okla. and London: University of Oklahoma Press, 1953.

Carley, Kenneth. *The Sioux Uprising of 1862*. St. Paul: The Minnesota Historical Society, 1976.

Catlin, George. *North American Indians: 1832-1839: Being Letters and Notes on their Manners, Customs and Conditions, Written During Eight Years' Travel Amongst the Wildest Tribes of Indians in North America*. Edinburgh: John Gant, 1926.

Chamberlin, J.E. *The Harrowing of Eden: White Attitudes Toward Native Americans*. New York: The Seabury Press, 1975.

Churchill, Ward. *Indians Are Us?: Culture and Genocide in Native North America*. Monroe, Maine: Common Courage Press, 1994.

Deloria, Ella C. *Dakota Texts*. Vermillion, S.D.: Dakota Press, 1978.

Deloria, Ella Cara. *Waterlily*. Lincoln, Neb. and London: University of Nebraska Press, 1988.

Erdoes, Richard and Ortiz, Alfonso, eds. *American Indian Myths and Legends*. New York: Pantheon Books, 1984.

Fire Lame Deer, Archie and Richard Erdoes. *Gift of Power: The Life and Teachings of a Lakota Medicine Man*. Santa Fe: Bear and Company, 1992.

Hammerschlag, Carl A., M.D. *The Dancing Healers: A Doctor's Journey of Healing with Native Americans*. San Francisco: Harper, 1989.

Hassrick, Royal B. *The Sioux: Life and Customs of a Warrior Society*. Norman, Okla. and London: University of Oklahoma Press, 1964.

Lund, Duane R. *Native American Recipes and Remedies*. Cambridge, Minn.: Adventure Publications, 1989.

MacFarlan, Allan and Paulette. *Handbook of American Indian Games*.

New York: Dover Publications, 1958.

McGaa, Ed (Eagle Man). *Mother Earth Spirituality: Native American Paths to Healing Ourselves and Our World*. San Francisco: Harper, 1990.

Neihardt, John G. *Black Elk Speaks: Being the Life Story of a Holy Man of the Oglala Sioux*. Lincoln, Neb. and London: University of Nebraska Press, 1932.

Neihardt, John G. *When the Tree Flowered: The Story of Eagle Voice, a Sioux Indian* (New Edition). Lincoln, Neb. and London: University of Nebraska Press, 1991.

Prucha, Francis Paul. *The Great Father: The United States Government and the American Indians*. Lincoln, Neb. and London: University of Nebraska Press, 1984.

Silliman, Lee. ed. *We Seized Our Rifles: Recollections of the Montana Frontier*. Missoula. Mont.: Mountain Press Publishing Company, 1984.

Standing Bear, Luther. *My People the Sioux*. Lincoln, Neb. and London: University of Nebraska Press, 1975.

Steinmetz, Paul. *Meditation with Native Americans: Lakota Spirituality*. Santa Fe: Bear and Company, 1984.

Tooker, Elisabeth. *Native American Spirituality of the Eastern Woodlands: Sacred Myths, Dreams, Visions, Speeches, Healing Formulas, Rituals and Ceremonials*. Mahwah, N.Y.: Paulist Press, 1979.

Utter, Jack. *Wounded Knee and the Ghost Dance Tragedy: A Chronicle of Events Leading to and Including the Incident at Wounded Knee, South Dakota, on December 29, 1990*. Lake Anne, Mich.: National Woodlands Publishing Company, 1991.

Walker, James R. *Lakota Belief and Ritual*. Lincoln, Neb. and London: University of Nebraska Press, 1980.

Wall, Steve and Harvey Arden. *Wisdomkeepers: Meetings with Native American Spiritual Leaders*. Hillsboro, Ill.: Beyond Words Publishing, Inc, 1990.

BILL CODY BIBLIOGRAPHY

Davies, Henry Eugene. *Ten Days on the Plains*. Edited by Paul Andrew Hutton. Dallas: The DeGolyer Library, Southern Methodist

University Press, 1985 (Orig. pub. 1871).
Rosa, Joseph. *Buffalo Bill and His Wild West: A Pictorial Biography*. Lawrence, Kan.: University Press of Kansas, 1989.
Russell, Don. *The Lives and Legends of Buffalo Bill*. Norman, Okla. and London: University of Oklahoma Press, 1960.
Sell, Henry Blackman and Weybright, Victor. *Buffalo Bill and the Wild West*. Basin, Wyo.: Big Horn Books, 1979.
Turner, Frederick. *Beyond Geography: The Western Spirit Against the Wilderness*. New York: The Viking Press, 1980.
Wetmore, Helen Cody. *Last of the Great Scouts: The Life Story of Col. William F. Cody, "Buffalo Bill," as Told by His Sister, Helen Cody Wetmore*. Chicago and Duluth, Minn.: The Duluth Press Pub. Co., 1899.

ACKNOWLEDGMENTS

A special word of thanks must be proffered to Paul Fees, head curator of the Buffalo Bill Historical Center in Cody, Wyoming. Paul and his staff graciously endured a wandering storyteller's three-day visit. Head Librarian Tina Stopka was most helpful in anticipating my areas of interest. Both gave of their time and willingly copied materials far beyond my expectations. Errors in my previous research were corrected. Encouragement was offered.

A word of gratitude to Chuck Eagler who interrupted a medical leave to speed me through the Center complex for some final notes.

Martha Kennedy and Jeanetta Drueke of the Great Plains Collection and Reference Library at the University of Nebraska in Lincoln helped me through a maze of materials in their Native American section and allowed me freedom to "stumble upon" treasures which shaped my sensitivities.

Errors in interpretation and judgment in this volume are strictly my own.